BLUE'S BOSS

THE EVERETT BROS BOOK 1

CANDICE BLAKE

1

BLUE

I fiddled with my tie while sitting down at the coffee shop. I was waiting there, across the street from where I had a job interview in exactly thirty minutes. The heat made my white button-up shirt stick to my skin, and I could feel a trickle of sweat roll behind my ear.

It was the third day of July and I just got laid off from my previous job two weeks ago. No one had ever fired me before. It felt like shit. I felt unwanted, undesired...*and my tie was still undone.*

Things were going well before this moment in my life. I thought I had it all figured out, and to be honest that was where things went wrong. I learned from my lesson, but I knew that I had to get back on my feet to pay the bills.

I took another sip of iced coffee as I scrolled on my phone once more. I was trying to find a proper YouTube tutorial on how to tie my tie. I looked at the time and I had thirty minutes left before my interview across the street.

I tried again for what felt like the millionth time. In the corner of my eye, I noticed a handsome man walk in.

That was an understatement.

How did he look so crisp on such a hot day? The sun hit his face with a golden sheen like it was sunset in Los Angeles. I forgot I was holding a tie at that moment, I dropped it and had to pick it back up again. On my way back up, I felt blood rush to my cheeks from the sudden movement. But it was also because I was standing in front of such a beautiful man.

Focus, Blue. It was not the time to be drooling over someone right now. I tried to turn my attention back to my phone but it was like my brain stopped working.

Short-circuited.

I couldn't turn my attention away.

He stayed at the front door of the coffee shop, looking down on his phone. It looked important. He commanded attention with the way he put one hand on his hip. When he finally put his phone away and he looked up, our eyes met briefly, before

I looked away. More blood rushed to my cheeks. He caught me staring and I didn't know what to do.

I clicked on a video on my phone and tried to follow the tie tutorial, wrapping the tie around my neck. The man walked closer and stopped right next to me.

His phone rang that familiar default iPhone ringtone. I was expecting him to pick it up so that I could hear his voice. But he'd silenced the call like it wasn't important enough to have his attention at that moment.

I was sitting down, while he was standing up, and he was waiting in line behind a woman pushing a stroller. He turned his back to me. I looked up again. *Like someone with no self-control.* Like someone who had the time to be staring at someone else right now instead of focusing.

But it was impossible.

His white shirt draped down his thick shoulders and strong back muscles. It hugged the small of his back and it was tailored to perfection.

I could smell his cologne. A strong cologne would usually turn me off, I much preferred the scent of a natural man. But what he was wearing had a woody freshness that reminded me of the outdoors. It contrasted the strong coffeehouse smell. His scent distinguished him from the strong muggy summer air outside as well.

The line inched forward, and he stepped further away from me. His scent drifted further away. In a way, I was a bit glad that he'd stolen my attention. Because my pre-interview jitters had turned into a lightheadedness. What was I saying? I still hadn't reviewed the notes on my phone like I'd promised myself I would.

I continued to make progress on my tie. I followed the steps on the video exactly like it was showing me. It felt like an accomplishment when I finally tightened it one last time around my neck. I looked down to see the masterpiece, and holy shit, *it was anything but that.* The knot looked huge in comparison to the half Windsor that I was attempting. Mine was lopsided, and the underside was longer than the front. *Oh god...I'm a mess.*

I was sweating even more now.

Was the air conditioner even working in here?

I was close to giving up.

"Grande iced coffee, black, please," the man in the white shirt ordered. His voice was distinguished from the soft rock music that was playing in the background. It stood out from the rest of the conversations that the people were having. Particularly because it was so deep, and strong.

"Of course," the blonde barista said, as she beamed a smile toward him.

I felt a bit of jealousy that she'd gotten the opportunity to talk to him. Why do some people seem to have it all? She was gorgeous and skinny *and talking to the most beautiful man in the world.*

I looked up again to watch him fish out his black leather wallet from his back pocket.

He walked to the side counter where he waited for his drink. That was when he noticed that I was staring again. This time, I couldn't turn away, and our eyes locked onto each other.

I felt like I had to say or do something, apologize for staring or look away. *But I couldn't.* All my motor functions were overcome with paralysis. I'd never experienced something like that before.

"Iced coffee, black," the barista said, putting the drink on the counter.

"Thank you," the man said, breaking our staring contest, to meet the eyes of the barista.

I tried to untie the knot on my tie, but I'd managed to deadknot it instead.

I looked at the time again and I hadn't realized that I should be heading out by now. It was fifteen minutes before my job interview. Although the office was across the street, I knew it was the right thing to do to show up ten minutes early.

According to my research, that was not too early to be considered rude, and of course, not late.

I finally freed the messy, haphazard knot from my neck.

It had to be my hundredth attempt to tie the knot and the smell of cologne broke my concentration again. It perked my head back up from my phone.

"You need help with that?" the man asked.

My jaw dropped and my cheeks felt hotter than the humid air outside.

"No, I got it," I said, lying through my teeth.

It was my gut reaction to say no, to spare myself from more embarrassment. I knew that I wasn't going to tie this tie within ten minutes anyway. I needed to leave the coffeeshop before I was late, which was worse than being tieless in an interview.

I glanced down from his dark brown eyes that pierced into mine, and looked toward a lopsided smirk on his face. Below his chiseled jawline, he had a perfectly knotted half Windsor. A hint of stubble covered his face. His tie was a deep blue.

"Stand up," he said.

I hesitated as I looked up to him. I wondered what he'd do if I said no. But his command made me obey him.

When I stood, I realized how much taller he was than me. He pulled on the two sides of the tie around my neck. His strength jerked me forward toward him and I almost lost balance.

With him so close to me, I took in his scent. His tongue stuck out to the side of his mouth as he worked on my tie. I turned my head to the side, a bit intimidated by his large size, and how close he was standing.

Yes, he was attractive, but he was also a stranger. I wasn't usually comfortable around people that I didn't know.

"Look straight, or I won't be able to center it," he said. His assertive voice made me turn my head back toward him. "You have to make sure this side is longer than the other when it's wrapped around your neck."

I nodded, trying my hardest to pay attention. But at the same time, I tried my hardest not to make a fool of myself in front of this handsome man who was tying my tie for me.

He continued to perfect the knot, while he instructing me with his deep captivating voice. He made one last maneuver and slid the knot toward my neck.

All I could think about was what I wanted him to do with his large hands. He had a minimalistic watch worn on his right hand, it had a white face and a gold dial. His thick forearms had a layer of dark hair that covered them.

The man pulled the knot toward my throat and I felt one of his knuckles hit the base of my Adam's apple and it made me gulp. It was not too tight, so it wasn't choking me. But it was tight enough that I felt put together. It was like the feeling of putting in the final piece of a ten-thousand-piece jigsaw puzzle.

I looked down at my tie, which I wanted to throw out moments ago, to the perfectly done one that was on me.

"One last thing," he said. He flipped my collar down, his hands pressed over it like an iron. "There."

I looked back up at him. "Th...thank you," I said.

His lips curled back up again to a smirk, then he glanced back at his watch. He raised his brows and nodded toward me, then left the coffeehouse in a brisk walk. The door closed behind him. My eyes followed him through the window until he disappeared from view. I didn't even catch his name.

I stood there for a moment, looking around me, and it was like I was transported back to reality, back from a daydream.

When I looked down at my phone, I realized that I only had five minutes left before the interview. There was no more time for anything, and I sipped the last half of my iced coffee. It gave me an awful brain freeze, and I raced out the door into the summer heat.

The teal glass and black brick office building contrasted the old red brick facades that lined St. Clair West. The building was four stories tall. It wasn't that much taller than the other buildings, but the bold color definitely made it stand out.

I waited for the pedestrian light to signal the walk symbol for me to cross. I had my phone in one hand to keep an eye on the clock. There was a couple of minutes left as I walked across the street and approached the sliding glass doors.

My sleeves were rolled up and the air conditioner cooled the sweat on my exposed forearms as soon as I walked in.

I approached the receptionist who was sitting behind a white desk. She had perfect glassy skin, and she had a slight smile and her eyes were cast down on her computer screen. I walked up to her and she looked up at me.

"Hi," I said, smiling. "I have an interview at two o'clock."

"Great, please have a seat, and I'll let them know that you're here."

"Thank you," I said.

I smiled to hide my nervousness, but I also wanted to make a good first impression on everyone and anyone I met. I walked toward the black leather bench by the window. My steps echoed on the marble tiles, and I took a seat. The white walls were a stark contrast to the exterior. White tubes of fluorescent lights lined the ceiling. Everything was white, and it reminded me of the watch face that the handsome man was wearing at the coffee shop.

There was a glass elevator shaft centered right in the middle of the room. The glass of the elevator reflected the midafternoon sun. It was a beautiful day even though I was nervous about my interview. The receptionist got on the phone and made a call to let them know that I was here.

2

HUNTER

"Our two o'clock is here," Marie said.

I looked at the time and I had forgotten about the interview.

"Where does the time go?" I asked Marie, the project manager, who I'd hired ten years ago and had helped me grow this company from the very beginning.

"I ask myself the same question every single day," I said.

"I'm surprised you don't have a bed in your office, considering how you never leave this place," she said.

I smirked. "This place is my baby."

I stood up and gathered up the resume that I'd printed off earlier. A recruitment company had sent us this particular candidate. It was the first time that I'd decided to work with a recruitment company. I had to do it after the bad luck I've had with the people I'd tried to hire for this role in the past.

I pressed the down button on the elevator and I could hear the squeaky gears. I'd bought this historic building about a year ago after deciding to expand and hire more people. I tried to do all the work myself, but I couldn't anymore.

I guess the people around me had been right. I was no longer in my twenties. My sleepless nights and workaholism had finally caught up to me now that I was thirty.

I looked at this candidate's experience and qualifications on his resume.

"I hope this one's the one, or else we're going to have to settle with the girl we interviewed yesterday," Marie said.

"I'm hoping so too," I said. "Why is it so hard to fill this project administrator position?"

"It's not a hard job per say," Marie said. "But it's repetitive. It requires that person to be organized, consistent, and attentive to details."

"Sounds like me," I said, smirking.

"If only we could find someone like you," Marie said.

I knew she was just sucking up to me. I couldn't blame her, I did have favorites. But my favorite employees were the ones who worked hard, not the brown-nosers.

I did a lot of the administrative things before. It gave me that control I needed. But after burning out from overworking, my friends and family had advised me that I should take better care of myself. I'd told them I went to the gym every day, but they didn't buy my excuse for overworking. I loved working and I didn't know how to stop. It distracted me from other things that plagued my mind.

I smiled and put my hand on the side of the elevator frame to let Marie enter first. I pressed the button and we descended down to the main level.

The doors opened. My receptionist, Kelly, smiled when she saw me. She stood up and walked toward the candidate. The candidate stood up as well to greet me.

"Blue, this is Hunter and Marie," Kelly said.

I reached my hand out to shake his. That was when I realized that there was something familiar about this gentleman.

When our eyes met, I knew that he must've realized the same thing.

"Hi...it's a pleasure to meet you," Blue said.

I smirked. "It's a pleasure to meet you too."

What were the chances? I had tied this boy's tie in the coffee shop moments ago and now he was standing in the lobby of my firm wanting a job. I guess he wasn't *really* a boy, he looked like he was in his mid-twenties. But his nervous flustered energy made me wonder if this was his first job interview ever.

I hadn't even realized that he was a potential candidate when we were in the coffee shop. It was so frustrating watching someone fumble to tie their own tie that I had to intervene before I lost my own patience. It was rare that I'd helped a stranger, considering how much I had on my own plate.

I decided that I'd keep my mouth shut about the tie incident, to spare him from even more embarrassment. He shook Marie's hand and Kelly escorted us into the boardroom in the back of the lobby.

Marie and I sat down at the dark brown maple table, and Blue took a seat across from us. My receptionist shut the door behind her.

"Did you have any trouble finding our office?" Marie asked.

"Not at all, it's very distinguishable from the rest of the buildings nearby," Blue said.

It had been my decision to paint the red brick black so that it'd stand out.

He wasn't making any eye contact with me. I'd been used to it my whole life. I was a big guy. I hadn't realized how strong I was until I'd shaken a female client's hand once. I fractured a bone in her hand from the force of my handshake. It was the reason for losing that multimillion-dollar deal and I wasn't going to make that mistake again.

"So, I see that you've come from a design background," I said. "Why are you interested in this administrative role?"

He looked down on his lap, as if he had the answers written there, then he looked toward me.

"I've been trying to move away from design, and into the project management space. I...I think this role would help me get there."

"So, do you actually have experience in project administration?" Marie asked as she was banging her pen against the table.

Marie loved to play bad cop during interviews. She said that was her way to make sure the candidate wasn't lying. It was a bit comical to me because of how serious she was.

Blue looked intimidated by it. I could see he was uncomfortable from the way he was pulling at his tie, the one I'd done up for him earlier.

"I did a bit of that in my last role," he said. "I worked for a small company and I got to do a lot of different things because of it."

"*Okay...*" Marie said. "But we're looking for someone who does one thing and who's good at it. What skills do you have that make you a good project administrator?"

Blue had become quiet. Marie was going to break the kid if I didn't step in.

I glanced down at his resume, and read the first few lines of his previous job experience.

"It says here that you've managed five to ten projects at a time, can you tell us a little bit more about that?" I asked.

"Yeah, sure," he said, sitting a bit higher in his seat.

"I was in charge of creating estimates for projects, editing proposals, and delivering invoices to clients," he said.

That was a good start. I was hoping that he was coming out of his shell so that I could decide whether or not he was fit for the role.

"What are three examples of inbound marketing strategies?" Marie asked out of the blue.

I glanced over at her, and she furrowed her brows. I glanced back over at Blue and his rounded eyes, unable to answer the question. The question was outside the scope of the job description anyway.

"How about this," I said, chiming in to break the silence. "Why don't you tell us what you enjoy about marketing?"

Blue took a deep breath, and his shoulders inched back in a more relaxed position.

"I love the idea of creating a pitch through storytelling. I love the planning and the brainstorming of ideas of how it can be marketable to consumers," he said.

Blue's eyes lit up and I realized he was named blue for a reason. His whole demeanor changed when I asked him that question. Suddenly, he didn't seem so tense. I looked over at Marie, her lips turned into a frown, and she crossed her arms. I could tell that she was not convinced that he was the right candidate.

"What do you plan to bring to this role?" I asked.

Marie clicked her pen against the table and started scribbling notes on Blue's resume.

"I want to help your company grow," Blue said. "I looked up the scope of your firm's work, and I appreciate how you work with a lot of nonprofit organizations. I want to be a part of a team who cares about social issues instead of only thinking about business."

Blue was right. I worked with nonprofits, but those were only because of tax breaks. It was all business for me.

"Do you have any questions for us?" Marie asked, cutting the conversation short.

Blue shuffled through some notes that he'd prepared. That's when Marie stood up abruptly.

"Thanks for coming in," she said. "I'll show you the way out."

Blue stood up as well, flustered at how fast Marie had walked to the door of the boardroom. I stood up to shake Blue's hand, and I was surprised by how firm his shake was for such a slender man. I'd always appreciated a firm handshake. From experience, it was a sign of honesty and a good character.

He left the room following Marie, and I studied his resume some more. We'd attended the same prestigious university, the same program even, and I didn't get a chance to ask him about it. Although I never ended up graduating.

Why didn't I speak up?

I was usually vocal about my opinion. But then again, I had a lot of trust in Marie, who'd been with me since almost the very beginning. Marie re-entered the room.

"What was that about?" I asked.

"He's not the right fit for the role," Marie said. "I could tell as soon as I met him in the lobby."

"How do you know that? We barely had a conversation before you rushed him out."

"Look, I was iffy when the recruitment agency sent his resume. His skills clearly show how he's a creative type, he has no place applying for an administrative role."

Marie was older than me. I'd never asked her age. I guessed that she was in her mid-fifties based on how old her children were and how long she'd been married. She'd gotten divorced last year. I'd always respected people who were older than me.

She was right to a degree. Our creative department was full, and we weren't hiring any more creative people any time soon.

"We don't have any more time to waste, we need someone and the work is piling up," Marie said.

She was right again.

"Should we call yesterday's applicant and send her an offer?" Marie asked.

I glanced down at the resume again, and I didn't know why I had such a hard time rejecting Blue. He reminded me a bit of myself when I was starting out in this cutthroat industry. Like

Blue, no one had given me the time of day when I was younger.

But I listened to Marie.

"Sure," I said.

We turned off the light in the boardroom and I headed back up to my office. It hadn't even been half an hour and I'd already gotten twenty new emails. We needed that project administrator. I crumpled up Blue's resume and tossed it in the trash can across the room. But I missed and it landed under my filing cabinet.

I continued to work away. I focused my attention on a multi-million-dollar pitch that I had to make at the end of the week. It was for a renowned chocolate company who was on an ambitious rebranding endeavor. It was my largest project yet, and somehow the fear of failing such a big project was getting the best of me.

I didn't remember the last time I slept for more than a few hours at a time. So, most nights, I'd opted to stay up instead. I kept working all night since I would otherwise be staring at the ceiling above my bed anyway. That only further fucked up my sleep schedule.

One by one, my employees popped their heads into my office to say good night, and by midnight I knew I was the last one to leave.

I hadn't eaten since lunchtime. It was my stomach that was grumbling that made me finally leave the office. I thought about how Marie was right again. Maybe getting a bed in my office was a good idea. Maybe even expand the kitchen. It would save me the time it took to drive back home to come back in a few hours later in the morning.

I went back down and left through the back door which locked by itself. Most of the restaurants on St. Clair were closed on Monday, so I couldn't even pop by my favorite restaurant. I looked to my left and saw that the pizza shop on the corner still had their lights on so I walked in that direction.

"Can you spare some change?" a homeless man asked, crouched on the side of the road.

I shook my head and continued walking. I knew I had money in my pockets but I didn't believe in handouts. I didn't get to where I was if it wasn't from hard work. Sure, some people were worse off than others. But the people who knew the life I came from have said that if I could make it, then anything was possible.

3

BLUE

It was the day after the most awful interview I'd ever had in my life.

I arrived back at my brother's apartment. I'd spent ten hours at the library applying for more jobs. Before I'd even taken off my shoes, I slammed my face down on the pillow on the arm of the couch. My brother's couch was also my bed for the time being.

I'd run out of money to pay my rent and I was evicted. My previous landlord was nice enough to let me get my things before he had me surrender my keys. I was already a couple months behind when I'd told him that I was laid off and couldn't afford to pay him. He was angry, but he also liked me as a person, so he let me off easy.

My brother Harry had gotten out of the shower. I must've surprised him by being home because he came out half naked with a towel slung around his waist.

"Jesus Christ, when did you get home?" he asked, running his fingers through his red hair to shake some of the water out.

"Just now," I said, so quiet and exhausted that I wasn't sure if he'd heard me.

Harry walked to the kitchen and opened the door of his fridge. The apartment was as hot as it was outside, and the heat had a way of making me lose patience for everything. I guess the Everetts were known to be a bit hot-blooded. Harry especially.

I yanked on the buttons of my shirt and took it off and tossed it on the ground. I would've taken off my undershirt too if my brother wasn't around.

"So, how'd the interview go yesterday?" Harry asked.

I sighed, hoping he'd get the message. But he'd sat down on the sectional across from me, taking a bite of an apple that was as red as his hair.

"It couldn't have gone worse," I said.

I told him the story of how Hunter, the CEO, helped me tie my tie before the interview without knowing that I was a potential candidate.

"Wow, you really fucked that one up, didn't you," he said, taking another bite from the apple. "I could've tied it the night before for you."

"I don't need your opinion on the situation right now," I said.

"Well, don't beat yourself up too hard, there's going to be more opportunities. You'll find something soon," he said.

"I sure hope so, and I hope I never get interviewed by a woman who was as rude as her again," I said.

"I thought he was a guy," Harry said.

"I'm talking about the project manager. She was practically trying to get me out the door as soon as I sat down," I said. "I felt like she didn't even give me a chance."

"Well, consider yourself lucky then. You don't have to work with her."

I was grateful for my brother's generosity to let me stay with him while I got back on my feet. Before that, I hadn't even seen what his apartment looked like since he moved six months ago

Even though Harry was my older brother and we lived in the same city, we never really hung out. It wasn't because we hated each other or anything, we just didn't have much in common.

He had baseball memorabilia from high school decorated on all his walls even though he had graduated almost ten years ago. There were even trophies from when he'd won the little league. He was someone who was defined by his past.

I kicked off my shoes to put my feet up on the couch.

"Put your shoes away," Harry said. "And don't throw your tie everywhere."

"Hey, will you let me be upset for a bit?" I shot back.

"Go for it," Harry said, rolling his eyes.

He stood up and threw his apple core in the garbage under the kitchen sink then retreated back into his room. He'd always had a bit of a temper, and I always thought that he'd gotten it from our mom. But he was old enough now to know when to remove himself from the situation whenever he got too tense.

He was right, though. I was a guest and I should at least be respectful if I couldn't even afford to pay him for letting me stay there.

I picked up my shoes and put them on the rack at the front door. I stripped out of my clothes that I hung up in the closet next to the winter coats. It was my temporary closet.

My brother returned to the living room with athletic shorts on and a white t-shirt. It looked like he'd cut the sleeves off himself to show off his muscular arms. They were much bigger and defined than mine. He plopped himself in front of the TV and turned to the sports channel to play the soccer game.

The voice of the sportscaster and the white noise of the crowd's cheer brought me back to a sad part of my childhood. I'd always felt left out, sitting on the couch watching my two older brothers and dad bond over the sports game.

There was a point where I'd stopped pretending I was enjoying it. My mind would drift to daydream about a cute boy at school or an art project that I was working on.

Needless to say, none of them were surprised when I'd come out of the closet. My mother had tried to at least pretend she was shocked. But I knew she'd seen the gay porno magazine I had left on my bed when I was sixteen. I came home from school and saw it sitting there and she hadn't made my bed that day like she always did.

I closed my eyes trying to forget my awful week. It was an awful few weeks really, ever since I lost my job.

But my mind kept going back to the moment I saw Hunter for the first time in the coffeehouse. Then, the moments when he helped me tie my tie. The shock in his eyes to have seen me again in his office. Why was I reliving these embarrassing moments? As if it wasn't enough torture to have lived through it once, I was now reliving them over and over again.

Harry, sprawled out on the couch, continued to watch the soccer game. I went to the dining table where I had boxes of all my personal belongings and clothes stacked on and all around it.

I was planning to throw away some things I didn't need so that I could free up a bit of extra baggage in my life. Plus, I had no business keeping all my things when I no longer had my own place for it.

I opened a box. I dug through the pile of unfolded clothes that I'd tossed in when my landlord was watching over me. I hadn't worn some of the shirts in years. I folded them on a dining chair so that I could donate them later that week.

The next box was filled with stationery that I'd once used in college. Between the pens and markers, there were remnants of design proposals that I created. The design proposals brought back beautiful memories of my college days. I'd graduated only three years ago. But it'd felt like a lifetime ever since working at that soul-crushing corporate job that I got fired from.

I wondered if everyone felt the same way about going to a nine-to-five job. The feeling of dread. Waking up at the crack of dawn. Watching the minute hand of a clock inch it's way to noon so that I could step out for lunch and get thirty minutes of sun. Then, trying to stay awake until it's time to go home.

Were people better at hiding the boringness of it all? Did people actually care about working for their boss who'd throw them under the bus any moment?

"Yes!" Harry screamed.

He stood up from the couch so abruptly that I felt the floor shake. A player on the team he was rooting for had scored.

I decided to keep everything in my box of designs and stationery. The things inside were still too sentimental to me to throw away. Being in school was the last time that I remembered feeling joy. It was as if I was sold a dream in school. A dream that I'd do what I'd love once I graduated. The reality was that I'd be stuck in an office doing things that other people didn't want to do.

I closed the box up and put it aside.

I opened another one. As soon as I peeled back the brown cardboard flaps, I realized which box it was. It was a box that wasn't mine. Or maybe a better way to put it was that it belonged to someone that fucked me over.

At the very top was a picture frame that was turned upside down. I flipped it over and it was a photo of Jake and me. It was one of those photos that were taken while on a roller coaster. Both our faces were flattened by the force and speed of how fast the coaster was going. My blond hair stood straight up, and Jake and I were holding hands.

My body felt heavy as I remembered how much fun that day was before everything turned upside down. I put the photo aside, and I could take in the scent of his clothes that smelled of what was formerly his side of the bed. I was feeling a flood of emotions, but I knew that it was for the better that things ended between us.

I put the picture frame back in the box and closed it up. This box was going straight to the trash. I didn't need to be reminded of him anymore.

My brother had turned off the television and he was slumped over the armrest of the sofa looking at me.

"What are you planning to do with those things?" he asked.

"I'm throwing most of it away and donating some," I said.

I ran a pair of scissors over the transparent tape of another box and opened it.

"We can use my truck if you need to bring it anywhere," Harry said.

I nodded and forced a tight smile.

"Hey, don't beat yourself up over it. People get fired all the time, and it's nothing to worry about."

"I know, I didn't get *fired*, I got *laid off*," I said.

"Same thing," Harry said, looking at his watch. "Let's get dinner or something, I'm starving."

My stomach growled at the thought of food. The only thing I'd eaten that day was a bowl of oatmeal before heading to the library. I was planning on making some beans and rice for dinner to save some money. But I really needed an excuse to get out of the house.

"Where do you want to go?" I asked, clutching my stomach. My legs were starting to hurt from how I was sitting.

"There's a new pub that opened up that I want to try. They serve Indian pub food and you know how much I like Indian," he said.

I hesitated at the thought of eating out, an activity that I couldn't afford right now.

"Come on, I'll pay," Harry said. "Just give me some company."

"Alright, I'll come," I said, getting up off the floor.

I pushed the boxes and stacked them back up against the

wall. Then, I took the clothes that I was planning to donate and put them in a large garbage bag.

Harry went into his room to put jeans on. He slipped on his steel-toed construction boots that had concrete specks all over them.

"You don't have a pair of shoes that you don't work in?" I asked.

"Who cares? We're just having dinner," he said, opening the front door and waiting for me to step out.

I wish I had that attitude—to not care and take things so personally. It would solve a lot of my problems and get me out of this mess.

We drove to the Salvation Army in my brother's truck. It was right before closing time. There was an employee who standing on the other side of the door making sure no one was walking in.

Harry's truck rattled as he slowed to a stop in a parking spot right in front of the store. I reached forward and turned down the volume of the annoying country music he was playing. Sometimes I wondered if I was raised in the wrong family. It seemed like I shared absolutely no interests with any member of the Everett family.

I stepped out of the truck. The air had cooled considerably since this afternoon. The sky was turning that golden color that reminded me of Hunter's vibrant glow.

I walked around the pickup truck, running my finger along the side and drawing a line through the dust.

There were two bags of clothes that I was planning to donate. I hadn't sifted through the other boxes yet and I knew that I would have a lot more.

As I walked toward the front, the employee had opened the door for me, and I smiled as I carried a bag in each hand.

"Blue?" she called back at me.

I looked up and realized that I knew her from somewhere. She was an older lady with round glasses that made her grey eyes bigger than they actually were. Her thinning white hair swooped to the side. She was about half my height, and it was adorable how she looked up at me while she held the door open.

"Do you remember me?" she asked.

I furrowed my brows. I was desperately trying to recall where I recognized that face from and I remembered.

"Ah, Mrs. Walker," I said. "I didn't know you worked here!"

I remembered when I met her, she had already retired, so she must've started working again recently.

"I started not too long ago." Mrs. Walker smiled. "I didn't know what to do with all that free time, now that my husband is healthier and I don't have to care for him as much."

I'd met her and her husband at the elderly care facility, about a year ago, when I was volunteering on weekends.

"Ah, I'm glad he's doing well."

"He's doing very well, and he's been gardening nonstop again which has been keeping him busy. We've always wondered how you've been."

I hesitated and I tried to keep smiling.

"I am doing alright," I said. "Things could be better...but that's life, isn't it?"

She smiled with sympathy in her eyes. Mrs. Walker looked down and noticed that I was still holding onto the heavy bags. They were starting to hurt my shoulders and arms.

"Are you donating this? I can get them for you," she said, reaching her small hands out.

I was sure that the bags were too heavy for her, so I shook my head and brought them inside.

There were still a few shoppers in the Salvation Army scattered among the store. A woman was slowly sifting through a rack of colorful clothes. A man was standing in front of the shelves of vinyl, looking at one in his hands. A disgruntled cashier chewed on a piece of gum with her arms crossed over her blue vest watching them. She shot her gaze in my direction like I was coming in to shop right before it closed.

"Over here is fine," Mrs. Walker said, pointing to a bin where I could put the bags of donated clothes. "We're sorting it tomorrow morning."

"Great, thank you," I said, shaking my arms that were numb from holding onto them for so long.

"You look tired," Mrs. Walker said, looking up at me with her rounded grey eyes. "I may be wrong...but I can sense something is off with you."

Mrs. Walker noticing that something was off surprised me.

"I wish I had your wisdom. I'm doing okay, currently looking for work, but I'm sure I'll find something soon," I said.

I hated sharing my problems because I knew other people had their own. But since she was being so kind, I didn't want to just brush her off like that.

"Well, we're hiring for a store supervisor here, and I'm sure I can let the manager know how great of a young man you are."

"Th-thanks, Mrs. Walker, that's very generous of you," I said, hesitating.

What would my parents think of me working at a thrift store after they'd supported me through college? I pictured my ex's smug smirk and what he'd say to me. *I told you so, I knew you were a failure.*

My brother honked twice and I turned outside to see that he was looking annoyed. He started his truck. The headlights pierced through the store windows, blinding me.

"I'll let you know if I'm interested," I said, trying to be as polite as possible. "My brother is hungry so I have to go now."

"Go on, Blue. I'll be here when you decide. You should come to my house sometime if you ever need anything. After all, you helped us so much when my husband was sick, we'd be more than happy to return your generosity."

I nodded, and she reached for my hand and held it in hers before I left. I remembered how she used to do that to her husband's hand while she was talking to him. She'd whisper to him and let him know that she was forever by his side. I wished that I had that person in my life who cared about me in that way, who would make sacrifices for me like that.

The teenager behind the cash register aggressively cleared her voice. She picked up the phone and she made an announcement over the intercom. "The store is closing in ten minutes. Please bring all the items to the register immediately, *thank you.*"

It was my cue to leave the store. I went back outside and back in the truck. My brother had his arms crossed.

"Sorry," I said. "Got caught up with an old friend."

"I could see that," he said without even looking at me.

He backed out of the space before I could even close the door and we drove off the lot.

Harry was quiet on the way to the restaurant. I could tell he was hungry. Whenever he needed food in his system, he'd get all quiet and I'd know to not say anything to set him off. I wasn't sure which restaurant we were going to. But when he turned down the same street as the one where I had my interview with Hunter a day ago, I couldn't keep my mouth shut.

"Where exactly are we going?" I asked.

"I told you," he said, sounding annoyed. "We're going to the new pub that opened up."

"Here? In this neighborhood?" I asked.

I looked around and recognized the familiar red brick facades. Seeing the office building where I had that awful interview replaced the feeling of hunger in my stomach with a feeling of dread.

"Yes, here," Harry said, he slowed down to a stop.

He parallel parked his large pickup between two smaller sedans. It looked like he was going to hit both of them, but somehow, he managed to make it fit.

Harry unbuckled his seatbelt and opened the door, as I stayed frozen in my seat. We were right next to the black brick building that crushed my hopes and dreams just yesterday.

The pub we were going to was a few doors down from the coffeehouse where I met the CEO without even knowing it.

I got out of the truck and hopped down onto the pavement.

"I *really, really* hope I don't run into the people who rejected me yesterday," I said.

I had to walk on the road instead of the sidewalk because I couldn't squeeze between the parked cars.

"They already rejected you? It's only been a day," Harry said, as we approached the pub.

There was a deep blue awning with three sets of tables back-to-back under it that were filled with patrons. Above the sign was the name of the restaurant, *SAVERA*, displayed as a pink neon sign. It glowed against the rich blue awning.

The pub was busy, as it was the first week of their opening. The hostess wearing all black approached us with a smile. We waited for the staff to clear a table of patrons who'd just left. Vibrant smells of spices filled the restaurant. The open kitchen was in the front of house next to the bar. It was a small space but they somehow managed to pack many tables in different nooks and crannies.

Harry ordered a beer and I opted for a glass of water. I didn't want to spend money on alcohol, and I didn't trust myself to have more than one beer if I drank that evening. I looked at the condensation on Harry's pint and the refreshing bubbles that rose to the top.

"You can have a sip if you want," he said, after catching me staring at it. I snapped out of it and shook my head.

I ran my finger down the menu, which was simply printed on a piece of paper with a list of dishes written in a fancy font. I watched as the servers brought food out. My eyes followed the decadent dishes that I knew I couldn't afford if my brother didn't offer to foot the bill.

Our server returned to our table. He was wearing a black dress shirt with his sleeves rolled up his thick forearms. His appearance matched the vibe of the restaurant.

"So...what can I get for you guys?" our server asked.

My brother ordered a couple appetizers and a main. I ordered the cheapest item on the menu, a starter salad which I asked if they could add a side of chicken on it.

"I'll check with the kitchen," the server said.

He collected our menus and left.

I scanned the crowd and noticed the hip crowd of business professionals. Even the people who were dressed casually looked put together. Everyone looked like they were having a good time.

I looked over at Harry who was on his phone, scrolling through girls on Tinder.

"Does that app actually work?" I asked.

"Sometimes I get lucky," Harry said, without breaking his concentration. He was only swiping right which meant he was interested in every single girl on his screen.

I laughed, rolling my eyes. "You can't be interested in *everyone.*"

"It's about quantity, not quality. The more girls I swipe, the higher the chances that at least one of them is interested," Harry said. "How about you? Are you seeing anyone?"

His question took me by surprise because he'd never asked me that before. No one in my family ever did. I assumed that they didn't care.

"Not after Jake," I said. "The breakup is still pretty fresh, and I'm not in a position to be dating right now. How the hell am I going to bring someone home to your apartment anyway?"

"Well, I don't mind," Harry said. "Just text me if you ever need me to step out so you can have the place to yourself for a romantic rendezvous. I'll go fuck off somewhere for a bit."

That was a very nice offer from him. But having to explain why I was sleeping on the couch wasn't something that I was interested in doing.

Our server came back and let me know that my order was approved and that the food would be coming shortly. I watched him walk to the front where he greeted a group of people who'd walked in. It was a large crowd of about ten people, and the restaurant had reserved a table for them near the front.

When I held my glass of water to take a sip, I nearly dropped it when I saw who'd walked in. There was no denying who it was. He took command of the restaurant as soon as he walked in just like he did in the coffeehouse yesterday.

4

––––––––

HUNTER

We had a lot to celebrate that evening, and it was the rare occasion that I got to leave work at a reasonable hour. I invited my whole office out to dinner at the new pub that opened across the street. But only about ten people joined us.

My good friend, Giorgio, opened this restaurant. He was trying out a new Indian-style pub concept. We'd been real estate hunting together a year ago. I was trying to find an office suitable for me, and he was trying to find a restaurant space suitable for him. By chance, we had scored a place that was across from each other.

"Is Giorgio around tonight?" I asked our server.

"Ah, you're a friend of his?" the server asked.

I nodded and took a seat at the head of the table.

"He just stepped out to find a bottle of wine that someone had requested, he'll be returning shortly," he said.

The server left us the drink and food menus. I could tell that my employees were hesitant to order alcohol with their CEO.

"Don't be shy tonight. We deserve it after all the hard work we put in to win the huge proposal," I said to everyone sitting at the table.

I knew that I was going to get a few bottles of wine. Hell, I'd probably consume an entire bottle myself.

I rarely went out, and whenever I did, it was business related or networking related. Even tonight, I was here with people who worked for me, who had to like me because of their jobs.

We ordered our drinks and food, and I noticed my phone ringing in my pocket. I'd ignored it a few times but when it ringed for the fourth time, I knew I had to check it. It was a client calling, a very important client. I knew I had to answer it. I excused myself in the middle of my creative director's jokes that I'd heard too many times.

I walked to the back of the restaurant, and in the corner of my eye, I noticed a familiar face. At first, I didn't think much of it, but for some reason, I looked back.

It was Blue, the handsome young man who came in for an

interview yesterday. He looked uncomfortable. I figured it was because he'd already seen me at the restaurant that evening.

He looked different in a casual t-shirt, and without the tie that I'd helped him with. He was avoiding my eyes so I continued walking. I wondered who he was sitting with.

I walked to the very back of the restaurant down a dark corridor. There were boxes of supplies stacked against the wall next to the emergency exit door. The red sign above made the dark walls glow crimson. The music that blared in the main space was dampened in the corridor. I could make the phone call without it being too distracting.

I could tell the client was pissed off as soon as he answered. But I bit my lip and tried my hardest to not say anything that I'd regret. I listened to him rant about a fee that we charged him for extra work we did, which he thought was unjustified. Some people are so entitled. I pressed my index finger and thumb on the bridge of my nose. I couldn't wait to drink some of that wine.

I tried to distract myself, zoning out from my client's aggressive tone.

"I understand," I said over and over again.

I moved the phone away from my face. Through the narrow corridor, I could see Blue, his eyes stood out even from far away. He was talking to the person he was dining with.

I thought about the interview with him. I liked Blue, but Marie had already made the decision to hire another candidate for the role. Since talent acquisition wasn't my expertise, I gave her the okay to do so. But I was still worked up over the fact that we were so rude to Blue, who'd done nothing more than come in for an interview. It wasn't the impression I wanted to give to anyone who'd come to my firm. Sure, I knew that it was strictly business, but I felt like I owed him something. An apology even. And I never apologized to anyone. It wasn't my style to say sorry, and I'd gotten this far without having to use that dreadful word.

"Are you listening to me?" the client asked, his tone had snapped me back to reality.

"Yes," I said, without thinking. "Listen, can I give you a call back tomorrow? I'm in the middle of something right now."

"We don't have any more time! Tomorrow is too late," he shouted.

"I understand," I said. "I'll check with my staff and give you a call first thing tomorrow as soon as I step into my office."

The urge to chug a bottle of wine was even stronger after that conversation. But I somehow managed to get off the phone. On my way back, Blue caught my gaze. I gave him a smile, which he returned, though I could sense that both of our smiles were a bit forced.

I walked back to my table where my creative director was still talking nonstop. I could tell everyone else was trying not to look bored. The good news was that our drinks arrived. The server had poured me a tall glass of Pinot Grigio which I tossed back quickly.

Food came shortly after, and the menu that Giorgio had come up with impressed me. We got to sample every plate and ordered seconds on some that I enjoyed.

The more wine I drank, the more I could relax around my employees. I'd never been good at making small talk that was unrelated to business. I'd always tried my hardest to pretend like I was interested in other people's lives which I never cared much for. If it wasn't about a new project or opportunity, I couldn't give two shits. By the time we'd nearly finished all the food, I'd drank a whole bottle of Pinot Grigio myself.

I noticed when Giorgio entered through the front doors. He was holding two bottles of wine, one in each hand when he walked in.

There was a trickle of sweat on his forehead, like he'd just been running.

"Giorgio," I called out.

He was walking quickly to the bar area when he turned to me and smiled.

He dropped off the two bottles of wine at the bar and told the server which table they were for. He wiped the sweat off his forehead and came back toward my table.

"Wow, Hunter. Look who finally showed up," he said, resting his hand on my shoulder and squeezing it.

"I thought I'd bring everyone from the office to come for the opening as well," I said.

I squeezed his hand which was still on my shoulder.

He pulled up a chair from the vacant table next to us and he pulled it up next to me.

"So, what do you think?" he asked.

I nodded and reached to take another bite of dessert that was still on my plate.

"I didn't know you knew how to do Indian this well," I said.

"Neither did I," he said, smiling then followed with a laugh. His raised his voice to talk to everyone sitting at the table. "I owe it to my wife's family who taught me how to cook traditional Indian cuisine which I added a Canadian twist to."

"Giorgio married a beautiful Bollywood actress," I added. "They met here when she was filming a television series."

I was one of the groomsmen at their wedding. It was set in the gorgeous Italian countryside at a winery that belonged to Giorgio's uncle. Of course, they had a second wedding in India which I couldn't attend.

Giorgio and I chatted a bit. We caught up on the new proposals that I was working on, and the one that we were currently celebrating. The night went on longer than I'd intended, and the last of my employees had left to go home. I ordered Ubers for them so that they'd get home safely.

Giorgio was only half paying attention to me. His eyes were on his staff and making sure that things were running smoothly. After opening three successful restaurants, he knew exactly what he was doing. I could tell that this one was already going to be a success. I kept a network of friends that were successful in the city. If I ever needed help with something, I knew I could turn to them.

Giorgio was looking on across the restaurant. A server and what looked like a manager were standing over a table. Giorgio was keeping an eye on them. While I was in the middle of answering a question he'd just asked me, he excused himself to go see what the commotion was.

They were standing at the table where Blue was sitting, and I wondered what it was all about. I'd forgotten that Blue was still at the restaurant after so many glasses of wine.

I watched the manager's concerned expression on his face. She explained the situation to Giorgio, then they stepped away to discuss it in the kitchen. I could see Blue's eyes, and he didn't look too pleased.

I got up from the empty table and leaned over the bar to ask Giorgio what was happening.

"Neither of these goons has money to pay for their meals," Giorgio said. "Apparently one left their wallet at home, while the other guy wasn't expecting to have to pay."

"What are they going to do?" I asked.

"Well, I told them that one of them has to stay behind so the other can go home and get their money. But the one who knows how to drive is too hammered to do so, and the other doesn't have his license."

I looked over at the man that Blue was dining with. He had bright red hair and his arms crossed on the table and he rested his head against it.

"It's these Belgian beers on the menu, I tell you," Giorgio said to his servers. "You are going to have to start warning our customers that they are twenty percent alcohol. They're deceivingly light tasting."

"How many did he have?" I asked.

"Two," Giorgio said.

I hadn't realized how stressful running a restaurant was. I applauded Giorgio for his ability to run three successful ones.

I looked over at Blue. He was desperately trying to shake his friend to wake up. His other hand was on the phone trying to get a hold of someone. It was way past midnight and a weekday. I'd be shocked if he could find someone to come bail them out before the restaurant closed.

"How much is their bill?" I asked.

Giorgio slid over the tab. It wasn't too much in comparison to how much I'd already spent that evening on my own employees.

"You know what? Just tack it on to mine," I said.

"No, no, Hunter. That's bold of you but we'll let these hooligans figure it out themselves. At least one of them is sober enough to do something about it."

I glanced over at Blue again, and he didn't look like he was getting anywhere. The boy couldn't even tie his own tie for god's sake.

"Just give me the bill, Giorgio. I'm feeling nice today."

Giorgio glanced down at the bill again, then up at the clock to see that it was almost time to close up.

"Why do you insist on paying?" Giorgio asked. "You don't even know them."

"Like I said, I'm feeling generous tonight."

He thought for a moment, his staff members were still patiently waiting for his direction.

"We'll go fifty-fifty on it, how's that sound?" Giorgio said. "You brought a lot of people to my restaurant tonight."

"Sure," I said.

I pulled out my card and paid for my bill and half of Blue's dinner. Then, I went back to my table to finish the rest of the bottle of wine. I was alone now. The servers had even cleared all the food and plates, and the only thing left was my wine glass. I enjoyed being alone.

I was sipping on the wine and drafting an email that I was planning to send in the morning. I noticed in the corner of my eye that Blue had come up to my table.

"Thank you," Blue said. "You didn't have to...I asked a friend to come to help us. But I appreciate what you did."

I smiled at how shaky his voice was.

"No problem. Thanks for coming by the other day for the interview," I said, pausing before I said anything further. I wasn't sure if it was appropriate to tell him that he didn't get the job. But I decided that I'd let Marie be the one to break the news to him.

"I'll know how to tie my own tie from now on," he said, twisting his lips to a slight smile.

His eyes softened when he smiled. Though I wasn't attracted to other men, I could appreciate a handsome guy. I was, after all, in marketing. Everyone knew that being attractive helped with selling a product.

"Why don't you have a seat for a bit," I said, kicking my feet on the leg of the chair next to me and sliding it out.

He sat down and his cheeks turned rosy.

"Do you drink?" I asked him.

"Sometimes," he answered.

I wouldn't have offered if it wasn't for the fact that there was still half a bottle left. I was reaching close to my limit. I knew I wouldn't be able to finish it all if I wanted to head into the office early the next morning. I called a server, who was wiping a table, over to bring us another glass, and I poured him some.

He took a sip, and the red wine stained his pale lips a deep red after just one sip.

"Who's your friend over there?" I asked, nodding my head in the direction of the passed-out young man.

"He's my brother actually," Blue said.

His voice was soft and quiet like his smile. I had to lean in just to hear what he was saying over the music in the restaurant. It didn't help that the restaurant had started blasting the music even louder. There were no more patrons inside besides us. They were closed for the night as they finished cleaning.

"You guys don't look alike at all," I said.

Blue had blond hair and blue eyes. He was much slenderer than his brother who had a thicker build and wavy red hair.

"We get that a lot. None of my brothers look alike, and Harry over there can't hold his liquor like I can."

I smirked. "You're telling me you can drink then."

He nodded and took another sip of wine.

"Don't be shy then," I said.

I poured his already half-filled glass to the brim. It was drops away from it spilling over the sides.

His eyes widened as I put the bottle back on the table and waited to see what he'd do next. It was fun to test him a bit because of how innocent he appeared.

He took a deep breath. Blue raised the wine glass slowly to his stained lips, and carefully tilted it back. He closed his eyes in the process. Goddamn, I hadn't noticed how long his blond lashes were, and if they were on a girl, I'd be all over that. I was always a sucker for long lashes, it was my weakness.

It took him a few gulps but he finished the entire glass. He even raised the glass high above his face and let the last few drops fall in his open mouth.

I clapped and smiled.

"It's not really something I tell everyone," I said. "But in my industry, one of the most important things to be successful is to be able to drink a lot."

"And why's that?" he asked, he spoke louder to accommodate for the deafening music, and it was Blue who was leaning in close to me now.

"Because my clients, usually CEOs of large companies, are insane. They party harder than frat boys in college, and the amount of alcohol they drink is mind blowing."

"So, my brother won't be fit for that industry then," he said.

I let out a deep laugh, as we both glanced over at his brother who was still passed out. A server was trying to wipe the table around his face.

Blue was funny and I liked that a lot. I knew there was something special when I'd met him the day before. And I knew it was a mistake that Marie didn't give him a chance. He was also starting to loosen up now that he had some liquid courage in his system.

"What are you going to do to get home?" I asked.

"Take a cab I guess, if we could even find one in this hour."

"Why don't you just take an Uber?" I said, suggesting an alternative.

"I don't have the app on my phone, and I doubt my brother has the app because he has his own car."

"Where do you live?" I asked him.

He hesitated before answering me. "Why?"

"To see if I can do something about it—" I said before pausing.

Why was I suddenly so eager to help? Yeah, I footed the bill because I felt like I owed it to him after that awful interview. Yes, I invited him to some wine so that he could keep me company. But there was absolutely no reason for me to do anything about how he'd get home.

"Fourteen Robin Drive," he said.

"Is that close to Dupont Street?" I asked.

He nodded.

"I'll order an Uber, your place is on the way to mine, so I can drop you off."

"No," he said.

"No?" I repeated.

"I mean, thank you for the offer, but I'd feel bad if I took anything more from you tonight."

I raised a brow at him.

"You're not taking anything else from me, it's on the way," I said, simply stating the facts.

"Seriously, I'll be fine," he said.

"If you say so," I said.

I couldn't help but smirk at the memory of him fumbling with his tie at the cafe before the interview.

"I should seriously go though, if I plan on getting home tonight," he said, standing up from his seat.

He reached his hand out to shake mine. I was yet again reminded of how strong his grip was when he shook my hand. In my experience, men who shook my hand the strongest were often the most trustworthy.

5

———

BLUE

Why was it seemingly impossible to keep my cool around Hunter? I'd always been an awkward person. I was aware of the fact that I couldn't string together a sentence without tripping up on words. Sometimes I couldn't even have a drink without spilling it on myself. Luckily, I was able to have the glass of wine that Hunter had offered me without getting it on my shirt that evening. I wasn't expecting to run into someone important, let alone the CEO of the top marketing firm in the country.

Come on, Blue, try to be as smooth as possible.

After shaking his hand, all I wanted to do was fall into his strong arms. Looking at his smile made me hotter than the summer heat. Touching his hand made the hair on my arms tingle, my knees buckled under the weight of my tipsy body. I took in the smell of his cologne. I wanted his large, rugged hands to paw all over my body.

Come on, Blue, be smooth remember?

His eyes pierced into mine, his gaze was more intense than I was used to, and it made me self-conscious. Why was he looking at me like that? It was intimidating, to say the least.

"Thanks again for the drink, I'm going to try and get my brother home now," I said.

"Any time," he said, simply.

He sat back down and he returned his attention back on his phone. He was perfection, almost robotic in how there were no flaws in anything he did. That made me even more curious about what secrets he had. I wondered what was hidden beneath his perfectly pressed suit.

I went back to my brother, and I felt a bit guilty that I'd left him there for that long. I wanted him to disappear at that moment, so it'd spare me the embarrassment of trying to get him home. But he was generous enough to let me stay at his place. It wasn't his fault that he didn't know the beer he was drinking was a lot stronger than he'd thought. The only thing left to do was to try to wake him up.

I asked the server for a glass of water. Everyone was busy,

running around all over the restaurant. They were cleaning everything and putting things back in order. The server didn't look pleased when I'd asked for something after they'd already closed. They were already nice enough to let Hunter pay since I had no money. If it wasn't for the fact that Hunter helped me, I bet that they would've kicked us out by now.

The server filled a glass from the tap and slammed it on the bar counter. I brought it back to my table.

Harry was snoring with his face tucked between his arms. I'd always wondered if he was allergic to alcohol. His cheeks were rosy like his hair and he looked like a tomato.

"Drink some water," I said, pressing the cool glass to his face, hoping that'd be enough to wake him.

He groaned and he turned the other way.

I glanced over at Hunter, who was sipping on his wine. He was looking over at me, making me even more self-conscious now that I knew he was watching.

I tried to use a bit more force, tapping my hand on his rosy cheeks. I knew he didn't have some sort of alcohol poisoning. This wasn't the first time that I had to get him out of a sticky situation.

Come on, Blue, think of something.

I poured some of the cool water down his back and watched it trail down his white t-shirt.

His eyes opened and he jerked his head back.

"Harry!" I said. "We have to go home!"

He blinked a few times, then rubbed his eyes. I was hoping that he was soberer now and that he was alert enough to walk out of the restaurant with me.

"I feel like crap," he said, in a groggy voice.

"I know, can we please leave before they call the cops?" I asked, the glass of water was still in my hand, and I was ready to splash some more on his face if he lay back down.

I glanced over to Hunter's direction and I noticed that he'd left. A server cleared his wine glass.

"Help me up," Harry said, reaching his hand up to me.

I grabbed under his arms and tried to hoist him up.

He weighed fifty pounds more than me. It felt like I was trying to lift a boulder.

I used all my strength to try and get him upright, and with some considerable effort, he was able to stand up.

We inched our way out of the restaurant. I kept my eyes peeled out the large windows to see if there were any cabs nearby. The streets were empty, and most of the cars that were parked on the street were already gone. When we finally made it outside, I was already sweating. Carrying Harry felt like I was trying to walk underwater while being shackled to concrete.

I glanced around looking for taxis. There was no one even on the streets, everything was closed for the evening. I'd have to call a cab company and wait for them to arrive. I knew Harry had his keys in his pocket, but I didn't have my license, I had never learned to drive.

I noticed a car that was parked across the street with black tinted windows and headlights on. The driver sitting inside made a U-turn.

The luxury black car stopped right in front of us. When it'd come closer, I saw the Uber logo that glowed behind the windshield. Harry's arm was wrapped around my neck and mine was around his waist, I was trying my hardest to carry him.

The back door opened and I recognized the shiny black dress shoes that hit the pavement.

"Come on, let's get you boys home," Hunter said.

Hunter stepped out of the car and took Harry's arm off of me and slung it around his neck. Hunter had taken off his suit jacket. I could see his strong back muscles flex in his white dress shirt as he brought Harry into the vehicle.

Hunter made it look easy. Carrying Harry out of the restaurant felt like dragging a pile of bricks in quicksand. But Hunter didn't even break a sweat as he brought Harry into the back seat and lifted both his legs inside the vehicle.

"What are you waiting for?" Hunter said, breathing heavily and turning to me. "Get in."

I obeyed his orders and I pushed Harry over so that I could get in. Hunter got into the passenger seat. He'd left his suit jacket in the back, and I held onto it. It was still warm from him wearing it all night, and though it was a hot evening, the warm jacket made me feel safe.

"Is he going to throw up?" the Uber driver asked, turning back toward me.

"He'll be fine," I said. "He's just sleepy that's all."

Harry was already snoring again, and he rested his head against the window. The driver reached into the side panel of his car and pulled out a paper bag.

"Keep this with you in case he throws up," the driver said. "The last thing I want to do is charge you a cleaning fee for making a mess."

I took the bag and kept it in the center console between Harry and me.

I glanced up at Hunter who was looking out the window. The

streetlights cast a yellow glow on the side of his face and his sharp jawline.

"Is this the correct address?" the driver asked, pointing to his phone.

Hunter shook his head and looked back at me, waiting for me to reply. I gave Harry's address, and the driver put it on his phone. The GPS on his phone directed him back to Harry's apartment.

It was a silent ride back. The driver was looking back periodically at Harry to make sure he wasn't throwing up. I tilted Harry's head back against the window so he wasn't moving all over the place in his sleep. I thought it was his job, as the older brother, to take care of me, not the other way around.

I couldn't stop looking at Hunter. The windows in the back of the car were heavily tinted, so I could watch him without being seen. I felt like a predator. He wasn't doing anything that was particularly interesting. But to me, his gorgeous face was more interesting than any movie that I'd ever watched. His chest rose and fell to the rhythm of his breathing. The bulge in his trousers looked like a tasty mouthful. I wondered if he was hard or if he was naturally well endowed. My own cock was hard from fantasizing about all the dirty things that he could do to me—that I'd let him do to me. Embarrassed that Hunter might see my throbbing cock, I used his suit jacket to cover it up.

When I was certain that he wasn't looking, I brought the suit jacket to my face to take the smell of Hunter in. The smell of his natural scent and the cologne made me let out a quiet moan. His expensive cashmere suit that was probably equal to a year's rent for me. I closed my eyes and imagined that I was holding Hunter.

"Does it smell bad?" Hunter asked.

I opened my eyes. He was looking right at me with a smirk on his face before bringing his attention back on the road.

I felt the blood rush from my cock to my cheeks, and I bet I looked as red as Harry's hair.

I quickly put his blazer back on my lap.

"No," I said, trying desperately to think of an excuse of why I was smelling his blazer.

Come on, Blue. Say something. Anything.

But no words came out, and he turned to smile at me as if he knew more than he should. The way he was able to not care that I'd been taking in his scent bothered and embarrassed me at the same time. I wished I had his confidence and poise.

We went down St. Clair West. The driver turned to the side street where Harry's apartment was.

The car stalled, then stopped right in front of the doors of the red four-story brick building. I sat there, not knowing what to do. Should I thank them? Should I tell them to wait so that I could go upstairs to get money for Hunter for dinner and getting us home?

"I'll help him up," Hunter said.

I was glad he broke the silence and made the first move. I figured that was the reason why he was successful in life, because of his assertiveness.

Hunter got out from the passenger side. He told the driver to wait a few minutes for him through the window.

Hunter opened the door on Harry's side. Harry, who was still fast asleep, nearly fell out but Hunter had caught him just in time. Hunter's biceps and forearms flexed in his rolled-up shirt as he helped my brother out.

I'd been staring at Hunter for so long that I had to remind myself to stop. I was embarrassing myself.

I got out of the vehicle, and I was going to help Hunter, but he looked more than capable of carrying Harry by himself. He'd hoisted Harry up in his arms, and it was a bit comical to see a grown man hold another grown man like a baby. I would probably get in the way if I tried to help. Harry was snoring so loud that I was afraid he'd wake up the neighbors.

Hunter walked to the front door, and I remembered that I

didn't have a set of keys on me. I reached into the jeans of Harry's pants to pull them out, and I fumbled to find the right one.

When I finally got the right one, I held the door open for Hunter to walk in. Hunter scanned the dingy foyer. I watched a spider crawl up the smoke-stained walls. I wondered if the CEO had ever stepped in a place that was this old.

Of course, I was used to it. There wasn't much of a choice in Toronto's rental market, landlords drove the rent prices high. The ones that were affordable were either really far, really old, or really dirty. This one seemed to check all three boxes.

"Where to?" Hunter asked, with barely any strain in his voice, while holding my brother in his arms.

"Upstairs," I said, squeezing past him, and leading the way. His heavy footsteps and Harry's snores followed behind me. We were lucky to be on the second floor.

I unlocked the door and I was glad that we'd kept the fan on in his apartment. It was a bit cooler on the inside than it was in the hallway.

"Should I bring him in the bedroom?" Hunter asked.

"Yeah, that's probably a good idea," I said, walking to turn on the light in the kitchen. The light cast a long shadow of

Hunter and Harry onto the dark living room. I led Hunter to Harry's bedroom, and Hunter grunted as he leaned down to put Harry on the bed. Harry sprawled his arms out onto the mattress. I didn't even want to look at him for all the commotion and embarrassment that he caused for me that evening.

"Thank you," I said, looking down onto the ground, standing in the doorway of the dark bedroom. Hunter was still next to the bed. I was afraid that he'd leave back to his Uber and that I'd never see him again.

"No worries, Blue," he said, in his deep voice.

The way he said my name made me want to run into him and hug and kiss his lips.

I stepped back out into the living room so that he could leave Harry's room. Hunter scanned the small apartment like he did in the lobby.

"Your room?" he said, sliding himself past the couch and the doorway where I was standing.

"My room?" I repeated, not knowing what he was referring to.

I was overcome with horniness because he was so close to me.

"Yeah, I don't see any other doors, unless you guys share the same bed."

"Oh," I said, suddenly knowing what he was asking.

I didn't have a bedroom here. The feeling of shame and resentment crept up on me for having him come up here in the first place.

I wasn't sure if I should lie or deflect the question. But when I'd looked up to him, there was a bit of concern in his eyes. His gaze was still intense as ever but I'd gotten more used to its intensity. I couldn't bring myself to lie to him.

"I was evicted from my last place," I said. "So, I'm here with Harry for the time being until I find a new one."

"I see," Hunter said. "Well, I'm sure that things will fall into place soon."

Before I could respond, I heard a noise outside the window. It was the engine of a car starting and the sounds of it driving off. Hunter and I walked toward the living room window and looked down below to see the Uber had driven off.

"Fuck," Hunter said. "I thought I told him to wait."

It was the first time I'd heard him swear, and the intensity of him saying fuck made my body twitch.

"You did," I said. "I guess he lost his patience after having to deal with Harry...I'm sorry."

"It's not your fault, don't apologize for it," he said.

He reached his hand out to touch my back, and I moved away at the unfamiliar touch, which made him jerk his hand back as well. I savored at the warmth of that brief moment. I wished that I wasn't so awkward, maybe it may have lasted longer.

"Your blazer though," I said, suddenly recalling that I must've left it in the back seat.

"What about it?" Hunter asked.

He turned toward me and leaned up against the window ledge. His beautifully sculpted ass rested against the window.

"It's still in the back seat," I said, reminding him.

"No, it's not."

Hunter pointed down to my hands, and I was shocked to see it was in my hands. I hadn't realized that I was holding it this whole time, I was like a child with their comfort blanket. I felt stupid, like a person who asked where their glasses were, then later finding them on their head. I must've been so attached to the smell of his blazer that I hadn't realized that I'd kept it with me.

He beamed a smile, and let out a laugh, and I couldn't help but do the same.

I handed it back to him, and it felt like I was giving away something that belonged to me.

6

HUNTER

I wasn't stranded per se, but it was a bit annoying that I had to call another Uber to pick me up.

I had a sneaking suspicion that Blue was interested in men after I caught him smelling my blazer. I'd even called him out on it.

I wasn't the least bit afraid of a gay guy who was interested in me. I leveraged it to my advantage often, especially in the creative industry. I'd never slept with a man, or even kissed one.

I knew that I could use my sex appeal to my own advantage, whether it was with another man or woman. Sex sells. It was just the way of life.

"Can I get you something to drink?" Blue asked as he stepped into the kitchen.

The apartment was small. I could see every corner from where I was standing in the living area. The air was muggy even with the windows opened.

"Sure, water would be fine," I said, rubbing my temples from all the wine that I'd consumed that evening.

How was Blue living like this? There was a pillow on the arm of the couch, and a fitted sheet that wrapped the seats. I presumed that was where he was sleeping. I felt pity, knowing that I'd return back to my penthouse condo that evening.

I checked the time and it was already three in the morning. I wasn't buzzed anymore but I was starting to feel a bit hungover. I knew I wasn't going to get any sleep that night. I'd promised my client that I'd look over some details of the project that I was working on.

Blue came over to me and handed me a glass of water, and I chugged it and put the empty glass on the coffee table.

"Sorry, it's a mess in here," Blue said, frantically pulling the fitted sheet off the couch, and offered to let me sit down.

I was hesitant at first. I didn't know why I hadn't darted out the door as soon as I realized that the Uber had ditched me.

But my legs were tired from carrying his brother, who was almost as tall as me, all the way up the stairs.

Blue sat down next to me, and he turned on the television.

He was flipping through the channels and he'd settle on the Food Network. Kitchen Nightmares was on and Gordon Ramsey's face appeared on the screen. He was on one of those tirades where his face got all red and he looked like he was about to explode. Blue and I laughed at the dish he was served. It was supposed to be a chicken salad, but looked more like something that'd be served to a dog.

Blue's laugh was contagious as we watched. We shared glances at each other whenever something funny would happen. Then, we burst into fits of laughter. I hadn't remembered the last time I'd laughed so hard. I'd always tried my hardest not to show too much emotion in the office, it was how I'd gained respect.

I didn't even remember the last time that I sat down to watch a TV show. I had a home theater that I set up but never used. It was refreshing to be able to relax for a change. I felt at ease next to Blue, and for the entirety of the show, I'd realized that I wasn't thinking about business.

When the show finished, I was reminded that I hadn't planned to be spending an evening with someone I barely knew.

I could feel the heat of his body next to me on the small couch. I was a bit surprised when I felt my cock harden in my briefs. I figured that it was because of the heat in the apartment that made me hard. Drinking wine had a way of making me horny as well. I tried to cover it up by putting my hands over it, and I was hoping that Blue didn't see it and get the wrong message. I tried to remember the last time I jerked off and realized that it must've been a week because of all the deadlines I had.

I reached in my pocket and pully out my phone and searched to see if there were any Uber drivers nearby who could pick me up. But I was shocked to see that the closest one was thirty minutes away. I was fucked. I let out a sigh. How the hell did I get myself in this mess? It was times like these that reminded me why I hated helping others. It always resulted in a huge headache.

"What's wrong?" Blue asked.

"I have to head into the office in a few hours, and I haven't even showered," I said. "I still smell like wine."

"Well, you can always shower here," Blue said, pointing over to the door to the bathroom. "It's nothing fancy, but Harry does have clean towels that you could use."

I looked at the time. Even if I called a cab, there'd be no point heading home. I didn't have much time left.

"You sure?" I asked.

He nodded. Blue headed into the bathroom and reached under the sink to hand me a towel.

"It's the least I can do," he said, bringing the towel to me.

I grabbed the towel and tried to cover my hard-on the best I could and headed to the washroom. I walked awkwardly while pitching a tent in my trousers. The strip of lights above the mirror blinded me and I had to adjust my eyes from the darkness of the living room.

I squeezed into the tight space and shimmied around the toilet just so I could close the door. I took off my dress shirt and hung it up on a small hook on the back of the door. That was when I realized that the door didn't close all the way.

I opened it back up and poked my head out.

"Does this thing close?" I asked Blue who was still sitting out on the couch.

He got up from his seat and came toward me. Blue reached for the knob and tried to pull it shut but he wasn't able to.

"Sometimes when it gets too hot, the door doesn't close all the way," he said. "But if you turn the knob a certain way, it should work."

I tried to turn the doorknob while closing the door, but I didn't have any luck.

Blue squeezed into the small bathroom to show me how to close the door properly.

"Like this," he said, with enthusiasm in his voice.

The bathroom was so small that his ass was pressed up against my leg. Somehow that only made my cock throb even harder. I was uncomfortable, to say the least, and it didn't help that I hated small spaces, especially because I was so big. On top of that, I was already shirtless, and the heat of the apartment had my pits and my whole body sweating.

He tried to turn the knob both ways, but it wouldn't budge.

"It's alright," I said. "I'll just close it as much as I can."

At that point, I was already annoyed that my night hadn't turned out as planned. I was going to have to work a full day after not sleeping at all. I was going to have to drink a lot of coffee to get me through it.

Blue backed up against me once more so that he could open the door and he went back into the living room. I closed the door as much as I could, leaving a sliver between the door and the frame.

If I was going to be able to get back to my client that morning, I didn't have much more time to waste. I couldn't afford to lose that deal after purchasing the new office building. On top of that, I still had to hire someone to join the team.

I stripped down to my underwear. I looked in the mirror and flexing a pose to see the progress that I'd made in the gym. I'd been pretty strict on myself about sticking to a workout and eating regime. The results were definitely noticeable. In the past few weeks, I had been focusing on my upper body at the gym, and my shoulders were looking broader than ever.

I reached into the shower and I turned the water on and took off my underwear. My rock-hard cock flung out. I turned away from the door that was left ajar. I was incredibly horny for no reason besides the fact that I hadn't jerked off in forever because I was so busy.

I hopped inside. Sweat that had clung to my body all evening washed away. I was glad that Blue had offered to let me use his shower.

Bottles of soap and shampoo lined the edge of the tub and I sifted through them to find some soap. I squeezed the cool contents into my hands. I rubbed it all over the back of my neck, massaging myself. It cleared away my headache from all that wine I'd consumed.

I knew I had to take care of my cock, as I watched it pulse wildly. I squeezed more of the soap and lathered it in my hands and then ran my hand on my shaft, coating its length. I groaned at the incredible feeling.

I always took cold showers. I'd read somewhere that it was supposed to make me stronger as a person. The coldness of the water and the warmth of my hands stroking myself had me close to coming.

The muscles in my body tensed up. I tilted my head back feeling the cold water run down my face, down my back, then dripping off my chest.

I was so close, seconds away from exploding. Suddenly, the temperature of the water changed from cold to scalding hot. I let out a howling scream.

Moments later, I heard the door swing open, and then the shower curtains pulled back. Blue stared at me with his large and round blue eyes.

"What happened?" he asked, his breath was short and heavy from rushing in so quickly.

"The hot water turned on all of a sudden and it shocked the fuck out of me," I said.

"Oh, I thought you fell," he said. "It does that sometimes, you just have to hop in and out of it."

He was so casual about it as if it happened all the time. But in my shock, I'd forgotten that my hard cock was still in my hands with soap covering it. Blue directed his attention down my body and he could see my cock in my hands.

My heart started racing.

I was used to other people checking me out in the locker room. But I was in a place that I was unfamiliar with. I was also caught in the act of jerking off.

His lips were pursed and his eyes moved up and down my body. His awe turned me on a bit. It confused the hell out of me that I was harder than before. I was getting turned on by the fact that I was being admired.

"You need anything else?" Blue asked, his eyes moving back up from my cock to meet mine.

"I could use a bit of help," I said, my heart beating quicker.

I moved my hands up my shaft to the tip of the head then back down again.

"What do you need help with?" he asked, his voice was shaky, and I was sure that he wasn't expecting what I was about to say.

"Why don't you jump in?" I said.

Blue couldn't have taken off his clothes any faster. When he hopped inside, the water had turned back to cold. Even he was shocked at how cold it was. I waited a bit for the temperature to fluctuate back to normal.

We stood at opposite ends of the narrow tub, waiting for the other person to make the first move. This time, it was me whose eyes scanned his body. He was well built, more on the slender side. I wondered if he was a swimmer because of his lean and long muscles. Baby blond hairs covered every inch of his body but they were so light that it was barely noticeable. His hands covered his cock which I could see was rock hard.

7

BLUE

My heart pounded in my chest, and I was feeling a whole slew of emotions that I could barely handle.

Hunter was built like a Greek god. His head was almost touching the ceiling of the bathroom. The jet of water from the showerhead splashed on the back of his neck and ran down his pecs and shoulders. His body was covered in dark hair, making his thick muscles look even more defined.

I wanted to run my hands down his abs, and up his chest, but I didn't have the courage to do so. I didn't know why he'd told me to come inside the shower or what he allowed me to do. I was still fairly dry and my back was against the tiles opposite of where he was standing. We faced each other like one of those stand-offs in a western movie. Only instead of loaded guns, we had loaded cocks.

I had my hand covering my own hard-on, holding onto it so tight that pre-come had leaked out my tip. Why was I so scared to show that I was turned on by him? Clearly, he was hard too. I shivered, I didn't know what his intentions were, and I didn't even know if he was gay. I only knew that we were both in my brother's bathtub. I was naked, wet, horny.

"I won't hurt you," he said quietly. His voice echoed softly in the bathroom. I wondered if Harry could hear us. But I assumed that he was so passed out that it didn't matter.

He took a step toward me, and he reached for one of my hands which was guarding my cock. He exposed me, but he wasn't looking down at my body, instead, his steady and strong gaze pierced into my eyes.

Our bodies were closer together, but we weren't touching.

Hunter reached to hold my hand in his. I was once again reminded of how large his hands were. Slowly, Hunter pulled my hand on his cock.

I could see that his cock was a lot bigger than mine, thicker too. I grabbed it. His girth was so thick that I could barely wrap my hand around.

"Goddamn, Blue," he groaned, tilting his head back into the water.

I ran my hand up and down his shaft, watching it pulse in my hand. With my other hand, I started stroking myself as well. Water splashed onto me off his thick body.

He kept his eyes shut, closing them so tightly that he had wrinkles in the corner of them. He didn't open his eyes once.

I stroked him harder, and faster. I watched a bead of pre-come leak out of his tip, dripping down on the tub. I wished I had tasted it before it'd dripped away.

As I stroked him harder, his breaths got heavier, his chest rose and fell faster and faster. I felt his powerful muscles contract. As I watched him tighten up, I could feel my body tense up as well. I felt that warm pulsing sensation in my balls. Then, ropes of come erupted out of me so suddenly that it'd surprised me. The water washed away my come that had fallen onto his thick hairy legs.

"Don't stop, Blue," he said, his deep voice sounded so needy.

I continued to stroke him. I could see both his fists clench up before he released, and his come erupted and it coated my chest.

He opened his eyes again. He looked like he was in shock and he was still breathing heavily. The scent of his come was powerful. I realized that it'd smelled similar to the inside of his blazer, only it was ten times more potent. It was piney and musky. The scent made me feel weak and weightless. I wanted to fall into his arms, I wanted to kiss him, and have his arms wrap around me.

I looked into his eyes, but he was avoiding my gaze. He turned to splash water on his face, giving me a glimpse of his gorgeous ass for the first time.

"I really have to go," he said before he peeled back the shower curtains and stepped out onto the bathmat.

He dried off quickly and I could hear the door open, then shut behind him.

I stood in the shower, looking down at my chest that was covered in his come. It was the only thing left of Hunter in the bathroom and it was still on me. I watched the water clear it away. I was filled with a sense of emptiness. I wondered why he'd left so abruptly and why didn't he look at me when I was jerking him off.

I stepped out of the shower and I dried off, wrapping the towel around my waist. When I left the bathroom, I noticed that he'd left as well.

The television continued to play in the dark living room. A hint of sunlight was starting to pool into the windows.

I looked around the small apartment, hoping for some clues as to where he'd gone. But the only thing that was there was his blazer which was still hung over the side of the couch. He must've forgotten it in his haste.

I lay down on my couch, naked except the towel around my waist. I was confused. Did I do something wrong?

I wondered if he was totally straight, and I wondered if his experience with me was his first with another man. I wanted answers, but I wasn't sure if I'd ever get any.

I started feeling painful sharp jabs to my heart. It was the all too familiar feeling of being rejected after a job interview. It was the feeling of an already broken heart after breaking up with my ex-boyfriend, Jake. It was the feeling of uncertainty of my current situation. I should've had more self-control. It was a bad idea to jump in the shower with Hunter, thinking that we could've been anything more than a hookup.

I woke up to the sounds of Harry opening and closing the cupboards violently in the kitchen.

I rubbed my eyes and looked at the time on my phone, and it was barely even 8:00 a.m.

"Thank you for the wake-up call," I said, my voice was raspy.

I realized that I hadn't even put on clothes after I'd showered. I had passed out on the couch after staying up all night.

"Goddamn," Harry said. "Do you know what happened last night? How did I even get home?"

"I'm so pissed at you," I said. "You caused us so much trouble last night."

"I didn't even drink that much. I have no idea how I blacked out," Harry said.

He was trying to find a lid to a container of what looked like some oatmeal. He hadn't even put on matching socks. His curly red hair was disheveled.

"Apparently the beer was a lot stronger than you expected," I said.

"What did they serve me? Absinthe? Goddamn, I feel like a truck hit my face, and now I'm late for work."

He'd made a mess out of the kitchen until he finally found the plastic red lid.

"Where do you think you're going?" I asked him.

"To work, you know that."

"Yeah, good luck with that," I said. "Because of your drunk ass, we had to Uber home last night. Your truck is still at the restaurant."

"Shit! Really?" he asked, his voice sounding defeated.

He turned to look at the time on the stove and tossed both his hands up into his hair.

"You better call your boss or something to let him know that you're going to be late," I said.

He shook his head and sighed. I felt a bit better because it wasn't just my life that was in shambles.

Harry went back into his room and I could hear him call his boss. I grabbed onto the towel wrapped around my waist. I got up to put on some sweatpants and an old green high school gym shirt with a worn-out tiger printed on it.

"What'd your boss say?" I asked Harry when he returned to the living room.

"He said it's okay, and to come in whenever I could," Harry said. "I'm lucky that I stayed for overtime last week when no one volunteered to do so. I think that's why my boss is being so nice about this."

He returned to the kitchen to grab his container of oatmeal and brought it back to the couch. He was about to sit down when he noticed Hunter's blazer.

"Is this yours?" he asked, picking it up and holding it out. He immediately realized that it didn't belong to me, probably because it was expensive and too big to fit me.

"It's Hunter's, he helped us get home last night."

"Who's Hunter?" he asked.

Hearing Hunter's name brought back the pain of him leaving without saying goodbye. Harry really didn't remember anything that happened last night. I tried to ignore his question, but Harry looked at me while eating his oatmeal waiting for me to say something.

"He interviewed me the other day. Remember when I said that I didn't want to go to that pub last night since it was across the street from my interview?"

Harry nodded, spooning another bite of oatmeal in his mouth. "Oh, that. Yes, I remember."

"Well, Hunter, along with his employees, were there last night," I said. "Someone had to pay the bill because you forgot your wallet. Then, someone had to take us home because you were too inebriated to drive."

"Oh," Harry said, looking down into the container as he dragged his spoon through the oatmeal. "Sorry...I swear to never drink again. I thought I'd have a bit, I didn't realize that it'd knock me right the fuck out."

I sighed, seeing the sincerity in his green eyes. "Whatever," I said. "I know I won't get the job anyway."

"Really?" he asked. "Was it that bad?"

I didn't want to tell him what happened after in the shower, and I was hoping that I could never have to.

"Yeah, it was that bad."

"He must've at least been a little bit interested if he remembered you and then offered to bring you home."

"What do you mean?" I said.

"Yeah, interested to hire you for the job."

I took a deep breath when I realized what he was referring to. "Trust me, he's definitely not interested in me. I'll just move on and find something else."

"Well, you still have a lot of time. You're still young, Blue. Don't think your life is over because of one setback. Hell, I took so many more losses when I was your age."

Harry was only two years older than me, but he acted like he was my dad sometimes. Sometimes he even acted like he was older than Gray, our oldest brother.

"Thanks, Harry," I said. "I appreciate it."

I was lucky to have a brother who was so supportive. I hadn't even told my parents that I had lost my job. Harry was the first person I told. He told me that I shouldn't tell Mom and Dad until after I was settled with a new job.

"Don't you have to go to work?" I asked him.

"Yeah, I guess I'll call a cab to get my truck," he sighed.

Harry finished his oatmeal and the taxi arrived moments later. I was left alone in his apartment. Recently, I've hated the feeling of being alone, especially since my future seemed so bleak.

I was left wondering who exactly Hunter was and what the hell happened last night.

8

HUNTER

For the first time in a while, I left the door to my office closed. I needed that time for myself. The last thing I needed was for someone to ask me a question that I couldn't process right now. I'd gotten a call from my client earlier that morning with a list of threats, and I had to patiently listen to his tirade. Sometimes I wondered if it was even worth the trouble with all this work for myself.

But what was racking my brain the most was what happened last night with Blue. I had thought I had myself figured out. I was confident and I knew exactly who I was. But how the hell did I make another man jerk me off for the first time in my life?

Sure, I knew people had experimented in their college days. But the rare times that I found someone to be attractive enough to deserve my time, they were all women. That all changed last night. It was like I was living in a different universe. What was the most shocking was how much I'd enjoyed it...how great it felt to be touched like that. It was different being touched by a man. It felt more powerful, more sensual even. The fact that it was forbidden, at least forbidden in my own head, made it even hotter.

What was I doing, though?

I put my hands over my face, feeling like a fraud. I didn't even know my own self anymore.

It was disheartening how quickly I left Blue's place after what'd happened. I treated him like he was disposable, like he was a piece of trash. I regretted it the moment I stepped outside, but it wasn't enough to turn back to go back upstairs. I couldn't face him. Not in that moment, not in that state. It wasn't going to be a conversation that I was going to have with him when his brother was passed out in the other room.

I didn't know Blue.

Except for the fact that we both liked watching Kitchen Nightmares on TV.

I didn't know Blue.

Except for the fact that his soft delicate hands could make me orgasm harder than I had ever before.

I didn't know Blue.

Except for the fact that he had a sweet, toned body that I didn't even get a chance to touch.

I didn't know Blue.

But I sure as hell hoped he was able to keep a secret.

I wasn't going to let a one-night stand ruin my reputation or my empire that I've worked so hard to build. It wasn't going to happen. I wouldn't let it, and if I had to silence him somehow, I wasn't afraid to do it.

There was a knock on my door, and it made my head spin even faster.

"Come in," I said, reluctantly.

It was Marie, who had her greying brown hair tied up into a bun. She had on a black dress that fell above her knees. She was at the restaurant last evening, but she'd left around midnight.

"Feeling okay?" she asked.

"A-okay," I lied.

She grinned at me, knowing that I probably looked like a mess. I hadn't trimmed my beard. I hadn't left my office since coming in that morning for fear that my employees would see me looking like that. Marie came in and sat across from me. I sat up, trying to look as professional as I could.

"I tried calling the candidate that was our top choice this morning, but she's not returning my calls. I tried yesterday as well," she said.

"Did you try to send her an email?" I asked, trying my hardest to not sound annoyed.

"Yes, and attached the offer of employment. I did it yesterday. But I haven't heard back from her."

"So, what are you going to do?" I said.

It was rare that I was that short with Marie because she was one of the few people who didn't take shit from me. But she was oddly understanding, probably because I was in such a disheveled state.

"Candidates who aren't interested are 'ghosting' their potential employers," Marie said.

"Ghosting?" I asked. "What in the world is ghosting?"

"Yes, ghosting. When they don't return contact without giving a reason why. So, we may never know if she's interested or not."

I imagined something way more sinister when I heard the

word ghosting. But I was happy to know that it wasn't too serious.

"So, what's the plan from here?" I asked.

"Well, that's what I came in to talk about," she said.

There was a reason why I closed the door this morning. I was starting to wonder why I'd decided to come into the office at all. I should've just worked from home that day. I considered leaving around lunchtime, maybe lying about having a meeting.

"Well, what are the options?" I asked.

"We can restart the interview process. We will have to invite a new set of candidates to interview. Or we can go with one of our other choices. If we restart the interview process, it's going to take a lot of time and money. I know we don't have a lot of time."

I shook my head. There was never a dull moment as a CEO. "We can't restart it. The person should've started this week. One of our major clients called me this morning to give me shit. On top of that, we're falling behind with our newer projects."

I had to make a decision that wasn't going to ruin the reputation of this firm, and it had to be quick.

I caught a glimpse of my reflection on the screen of my

laptop. The circles under my eyes were dark and I knew I needed rest. I couldn't wait to get home so that I could shave and clean myself up properly.

In Marie's hands were the resumes of the people we interviewed and she laid them out on my desk. There were only three resumes, and I knew we had four people who came in.

I scanned them and I remembered Blue, whose resume wasn't there.

"Where's Blue's resume?" I asked Marie.

"God, do you really want to hire him? He's completely unfit for the role. I don't think he's mature enough to handle this position, he'll run us to the ground."

I looked at the names of the other people, and none of them were immediately recognizable. They were not memorable. But even prior to what had happened last night, I thought Blue was different from the rest.

"Let me think about it, Marie, I'll get back to you tomorrow."

She nodded and smiled tightly, then retrieved the papers and headed out of my office.

I wondered if I should give Blue a try for this role. I could put him on a three-month probation, and if he doesn't do a good job, I could fire him.

What was I doing, though?

I knew it was trouble to offer him a job, especially after what'd happened last night. It wasn't like I needed more stress for myself. But seeing him live on his brother's couch, and seeing how hard he was trying to make ends meet, made me think of me. I thought of the lowest point in my life. Nobody gave me the time of day when I was starting out in this cutthroat industry.

I had always had the philosophy of business is business, and I was good at keeping my emotions out of it. But with Blue, it was a different story, and I wondered if I'd regret it if I hired just another person to take this job. I wondered what Blue had to offer to me and my company.

I knew I was in a manic state from my lack of sleep, but I didn't want to hold off on this decision any further. It was time to go home even though it wasn't even noon yet. I put my laptop in my briefcase and turned off the lights in my office. On my way out, I went to Marie's desk.

"Please give Blue an offer of employment and see what his response is," I said to Marie.

Marie's eyes widened like I'd gone full-on crazy. She was probably right.

"You sure?" she asked, scratching her head, and then running her palms over her hair to smooth it out.

"Of course, I'm sure," I said.

I hated when people asked me that.

My decisions were always final, and I wouldn't say something that I didn't mean.

"Alright then, I'm warning you, this is going to spell trouble."

"I am going to head out for the rest of the day, so give me a call if you have any updates," I said.

I left the office without saying goodbye to anyone and I took a cab back to my condo.

I looked out the window of the back seat of the taxi. The sun was hitting the windows of the tall office buildings. It reminded me of Blue's tanned golden skin and the fine blond hair that covered his body. I was shocked by how I was thinking of Blue. I tried to clear my mind, paying attention to the people on the streets instead. It was around noon, so people in suits were perched against the sides of buildings eating their lunch. Some were on their phones smoking cigarettes.

There were so many people who were more suited for the role than Blue. But I didn't want anyone else. I knew I had to figure him out so that I could figure myself out. If I hired him and actually got to know him, I would know for sure that what happened last night was simply a mistake.

I shifted my attention toward a blonde woman, wearing a purple dress, walking down the street. I looked at how the dress curved off her ass, and her smooth toned legs glistened in the sun. But still, I couldn't get my mind off Blue. Even a hot woman wasn't comparable to Blue's seductive charm or the innocence of his laugh. Fuck.

The taxi took me east of the city and dropped me off at my condominium that had been revitalized from a bank.

I had purchased the unit five years ago before it was even up for sale to the public. The director of the real estate firm was a good friend of mine. He'd pulled some strings to let me buy the first unit. When I saw the penthouse suite, I knew it was the one I wanted. I requested to have the whole floor to myself. It was denied at first until they saw the check I was willing to sign. I fell in love with the bank vault that was eventually converted into my bedroom. I'd always loved how I could close the heavy concrete doors so that it could block the quietest sounds in the city.

I took a deep breath as soon as I stepped into my home. I dropped my briefcase on my kitchen counter, and went into my bedroom, falling right into my bed. The satin sheets wrapped around my body, and I closed my eyes. In my room, the silence and the darkness consumed me, and it felt as if I was in a vacuum, far away from the outside world.

I was exhausted, but thinking about Blue working in my office kept me awake. Thinking of his excitement made me smile. Blue would be happy to realize that he wouldn't have to sleep on his brother's couch.

But then, I wondered if it had been a mistake to make such a big decision in my tired and hungover state. I wouldn't know what to do about seeing him every day. I'd be distracted with him around.

9

BLUE

The St. Clair West streetcar made a squeaky sound as it glided along the tracks. I slid open the window, letting in a gentle breeze. I was making my way to the Salvation Army.

I'd called Mrs. Walker and she told me the manager offered me the job after the good things she had to say about me. The job paid not more than a dollar over minimum wage, but I wasn't in a position to ask for more. Plus, it wasn't like I was having any luck finding anything else. I wanted to start giving Harry some money to help with rent. Besides, it was for the Salvation Army, so I saw it as a good deed for the community anyway. Even so, I hoped to save up enough to get a place by the end of summer.

I got off at my stop and crossed the street to the one-story brick building. Shopping carts scattered the parking lot. There were a group of old men seated on the bench in front of the store smoking cigarettes. They were looking in one direction as if they were waiting for someone to arrive. I looked at my phone and realized that it was twenty minutes before I was asked to show up for my first day. But I'd arrived earlier in case there were any hang-ups taking the transit system. It always seemed to be delayed or not in service.

I walked past the three old men who turned their heads toward me. I waved and smiled, and they returned the gesture. Taking a deep breath, I stepped into the store. The automatic doors swung open, and a country song was playing over the PA system. The smell of thrift stores always reminded me of Grandma's house growing up.

I looked around to see if Mrs. Walker was there. Sure enough, she was standing near the ceramic aisle with a shopping cart of merchandise in front of her. She was putting some teal plates back on the shelf. Mrs. Walker had a smile on her face. I recognized that smile from the days when she was in the hospital with Mr. Walker, who was sick at the time. Her smile was a calm reassurance that everything was going to be alright. At least, I hoped so.

I approached her, and she'd been so concentrated in what she was doing that she didn't see me at first.

"Mrs. Walker," I said, waving at her.

"Blue! You made it," she said.

I smiled, and she came up to hug me like she always had whenever I showed up at the hospital to volunteer.

Mrs. Walker put one last cup on the shelf.

"Blue," she greeted. "I'll bring you to the back room so you can meet the general manager of the store. She'll help you get started."

We walked toward the back of the store. I ran my hand past a rack of winter jackets. Mrs. Walker brought me through the double doors to a small warehouse. It was piled high with donations. It was overwhelming to see so many things everywhere. There were boxes of clothes next to children's toys. Then, kitchen appliances with tangled cords on top of computer accessories. Beside that were old wooden chairs stacked next to dog carriers.

Nervous about meeting the manager, I took a deep breath, but I ended up inhaling dust that sent me into a sneezing fit.

"Are you alright?" Mrs. Walker asked.

I nodded, even though I wasn't alright.

Seeing all these things around me made me think of the boxes that I had at Harry's apartment. I feared that I would never be able to get back on my feet and move out. I imagined the boxes multiplying until it took up the entire apartment. I wiped my sweaty palms on the side of my black pants, which I had been told to wear.

We finally made it to the office. A bronze tag hung crookedly on the door that read GENERAL MANAGER. The door was left open, and a large woman sat behind a computer. Her glasses reflected the computer screen. Though we were facing her, she didn't acknowledge us, even when we stepped inside.

"This is Blue," Mrs. Walker said, turning toward me with a smile. "He's the young man I was telling you about."

The manager glanced up at me with her painted fingernails that made a clicking sound as she typed on her keyboard. I smiled, trying my best to look excited about the new job, despite how I was feeling on the inside.

"Have a seat," she said, then turning to Mrs. Walker. "I'll take it from here, thank you. Please close the door."

"Good luck," Mrs. Walker whispered, before leaving the room.

I waited a few more minutes for the manager to finish whatever she was typing. She finally turned to me and eyed me up and down. Then, she swiveled her chair and rummaged through a box, pulling out a blue vest and tossed it in my direction. I caught it before it hit me in the face.

"I'm Blue," I said.

I reached out to shake her hand. But she looked at my hand as if they were dirty and shook her head. I retreated my hand back and put it in my lap.

"Put the vest on," she said, without introducing herself.

I looked at the vest which looked way too big but I put it on over my white t-shirt, and of course, I was right.

"It's all we have until we order more," she said. "You'll have to wear it for the time being."

After graduating at the top of my class, I couldn't believe that I was going to be working at a thrift store. On top of that, my manager didn't even seem interested in getting to know me. The smile I had when I first entered the room faded away. I was losing my enthusiasm for my first day of work.

"I'm going to have you organize our warehouse, for at least the first couple weeks. I want you to get an idea of the layout of the entire store," she said.

I looked at her and my eyes widened.

"Oh," I said quietly.

"What?" she asked. "You're too good for it?"

"No, it's not that. I thought the job was going to be more front facing, Mrs. Walker had told me it was going to be a supervisor position."

"Well," she said. "You seem a bit young, so we're going to have to see. All new hires spend the first few weeks in the warehouse."

I felt lied to. I wished I had the courage to walk out and hand her back the vest that was too big for me anyway. But the pain in my neck reminded me that I couldn't sleep on Harry's couch much longer. Beggars can't be choosers.

"Okay." I nodded.

She got up and she led me out to the warehouse.

"I need you to organize everything by category," she said, pointing to pieces of paper that were taped on the wall.

There were at least fifty categories that spanned the length of the warehouse. I felt overwhelmed, I couldn't even organize my own things let along things that didn't even belong to me.

"You have any questions?" she asked.

I shook my head, looking down the endless piles of things. Some boxes were stacked so high that I wondered how I was even going to reach it without it toppling over on me. My breaths got more and more shallow, and I felt like the walls were starting to narrow in. The feeling of claustrophobia was overwhelming. But I tried to remind myself that it was all in my head.

The manager went back into her room and closed the door so hard that it made me jump.

I looked up and down the warehouse. The lights were turned off in the back, so it looked like the piles of things went on forever into the void.

I felt alone, and I wondered how long it'd take me to finish it. Maybe this was a sort of probation, to see if I really wanted the job. Maybe I only had to do it for one day before the manager would come out and tell me that I passed the test. But I knew that I was only trying to make myself feel better.

I hoped for Mrs. Walker to walk through the two-way doors and offer some guidance on even where or how to start.

There was a teddy bear that was right next to me that reminded me of one I had when I was a kid. I held onto it as I walked between the mountains of things, looking for its appropriate home. Did it belong in Kids Toys or Play Room? Confused, I put it between both piles. One down, a thousand more to go.

I felt a vibration in my pocket. I'd put my phone on silent this morning so that I wasn't tempted to check it on my first day of work. But I could use a distraction. I walked down to the end of the warehouse, far away from the manager's office. I reached into my pocket to see that an unknown number was calling me.

"Hello?" I said, trying to be as quiet as possible.

"Hello?" the person on the other line said. "Can you hear me?"

There was an exit door by me, and I opened it, hoping to get more reception. It worked.

"Hi, is this Blue?" she asked.

"Yes, speaking," I said.

"It's Marie. I'm calling on behalf of Hunter to let you know that we want to offer you the position of Project Administrator. Are you still interested? And how soon can you start?'

I was still adjusting to the bright sunlight and the shock of what I was hearing. Coming from the dark warehouse, it'd felt like I had broken out of prison.

"Yes!" I said. "I'm very interested. I can start as soon as possible."

"Great, I'll send the offer to your email. Please sign it as soon as you can. We want you to start on Monday."

Tears filled my eyes.

"Thank you," I said.

"You're welcome," she said before she hung up.

In my excitement, I'd closed the exit door, and I realized that it was locked from the outside. I was tempted to go home. But I walked around the store, taking off the oversized blue vest that fit more like a hospital gown.

I went around to the front of the store and saw Mrs. Walker. She was in the vinyl record section, talking to a customer. I let her finish her conversation before I told her the news that I'd received on the phone.

"Well, congrats," she said. "Don't worry about this job. We'll find someone else. I know you're still young, and you owe no one anything. I knew that you wouldn't be here long, but I wanted to give you a bit of hope."

She reached out toward my vest and took it from me. "Don't worry about telling the GM. I'll do it for you," Mrs. Walker said.

I smiled and gave her a hug.

She put her small, frail hands on my cheeks. "Come by for dinner one day. Mr. Walker will be so happy to see you!"

"I will for sure," I said, I realized that my cheeks were wet from my own tears.

I'd never felt more excited to leave a job. But I was confused. Why did Hunter want to hire me after what happened at Harry's apartment the other night?

10

HUNTER

I was looking forward to this Monday more than any other, and I knew the reason why. It was because it was Blue's first day, and I knew it'd be special. I arrived earlier than everyone else, which wasn't uncommon. But feeling this awake and alive even before my first cup of coffee was unusual. I was pacing around my office with a huge smile on my face without realizing it.

To distract myself, I looked over a batch of emails that'd accumulated over the weekend. I hadn't felt this anxious in a while. The feeling was similar to the moment right before I stepped into a boardroom to make a sales pitch. Yet, there was hardly any good reason that I should be feeling this way. Blue, after all, was nothing more than someone that I had just hired.

The thought of seeing Blue again made my heart race quicker. The only thing that could distract me was to head downstairs to see the employees who'd arrived.

"Hunter, you're looking like you're a bit happier than usual today," Portia, one of the designers, said to me.

I hadn't even realized that I was smiling and pacing back and forth again. I wiped the smile off my face.

"Just thinking about work things," I said, shrugging.

I'd even put on my favorite suit. It was a blue and gold pinstripe one. I only wore it during special occasions like when I was meeting a head honcho at another firm. Oddly enough, today seemed like the proper occasion to look as sharp as I could. I wanted Blue to know who was the boss around here, in case he didn't already know.

When I returned to my office, I got a call from my reception-ist, letting me know that Blue was coming up to see me. I sat behind my desk, pretending to act busy, when I'd barely looked at the work I had to do that day.

There was a knock on my door.

"Come in," I said.

The door opened and Blue's face poked in. He looked at me with his crystal eyes that made it hard for me to turn away.

I stood up and walked around my desk to shake his hand. I was reminded of the strength of his grip. His right hand was the same one that'd stroke my cock, making me erupt all over his chest in the shower. I tried my hardest to remain professional, but we both knew what we did together. We both had a secret that we had to keep.

He was wearing grey trousers that were cropped at his ankle, revealing a pair of bright teal socks. His white dress shirt was tucked in, and he was wearing the same blue tie as when I'd first met him. He put his hand on his tie and flattened it against his shirt. He had on a smile that beamed ear to ear as if he was proud of the fact that he'd put his own tie on. It had an effect on me. I tried to keep a straight face, I couldn't help but at least show a bit of a smirk at his enthusiasm on his first day of work.

I gestured for him to take a seat across from me.

"Welcome, Blue. How do you feel about your first day?" I asked.

"I'm excited, I wanted to say thank you for believing in me," Blue said, looking down onto his lap.

"Well, it's not going to be an easy job, and the people in this industry will skin you alive if you don't prove yourself early. So, don't think it's going to be easy. But...I'm sure you'll be able to prove them wrong and make me proud."

"I know," Blue said. "I'll try my best."

"Good," I said. "You'll be reporting to Marie, she's on the third floor and she's expecting you now, so you better get going."

He nodded and stood up.

"One last thing," I said. "I'm hoping that you're aware that what happened in the past should be kept a secret—"

"Don't worry, I won't say a thing," Blue said, interrupting what I had to say.

"One more thing," I said. "It's a tradition that I take new hires out to lunch for the first day. So, come into my office around noon, and we'll head out to eat somewhere."

"Great." He smiled.

When he turned to leave, I eyed his gorgeous plump ass. I'd always been an ass man, but I'd never in my life looked at another man's ass and have been turned on by it. Blue was giving me firsts for everything. It was impossible for me to look away until he finally disappeared from view. Why did I want to run my hands over his bronze skin?

I never second-guessed myself, but I wondered if it was a mistake to hire him. I knew he was going to be a distraction. I pictured Blue's outfit, his smile, his bronze skin, and his golden hair. Daydreaming about him stole all my attention away that morning. I'd rarely ever had another person occupy so much brain power. Should I have trusted my instinct, which was to never see him again after I'd left his brother's apartment?

I sighed, bringing my hands up to my face and putting them over my eyes. I hoped that lunch wasn't going to be awkward. But I've had enough lunches with people much more important than Blue to know how to handle myself. It was going to be business as usual. The purpose was to let them know the values of my company, what we strived to do, and what we represented. So, there would be no room for any nonsense and there was nothing to discuss other than work-related things.

I looked at the stack of papers on my desk that needed my attention. Finally, I got to work. It had always been a good method to distract myself from the constant stream of thoughts running through my head. I started by reviewing an important proposal.

Before I knew it, it was noon. I filed away the proposal I was working on, and I waited for Blue to come up for our lunch meeting. Waiting for him felt like time had frozen still. Noon became quarter past noon, then half past, and I couldn't wait any longer.

I went down the elevator to the third floor to see Blue sitting at his new desk. The cubicle was empty except for Blue's backpack hanging on the wall. Blue was leaning forward, looking at the computer screen.

"You're going to go blind if you get any closer," I said.

He turned and shifted a bit in his chair, he looked startled that I was watching him.

"Oh shit! I didn't know it was lunchtime," he said, standing up right away. "I'll let Marie know that I'll be leaving with you."

"No need, I already told her," I said. "Come on, I'm starving."

I was annoyed that I told Blue to come up at noon but he'd forgotten. Time management was a crucial part of his job, and I worried that he didn't have that kind of punctuality.

We made our way down to the lobby, and I showed him the binder where he needed to sign out. We went through the front doors to where I'd parked my car.

Blue climbed into the passenger seat.

"What do you want to eat?" I asked him.

Usually, it was up to me on where I'd take a new hire, depending on what I was feeling that day. But for some reason, I'd felt more easygoing that afternoon, so I let Blue decide.

"Do you like McDonald's?" he asked.

"What? You want to go to McDonald's for lunch?"

He looked at me, brows raised as if I was the crazy one.

"Why not?" Blue asked, reaching to put on his seatbelt.

"Well, I was thinking of a place that's...classier. But if you want McDonald's...we can go there," I said.

"Everyone likes McDonald's," he said.

"I haven't been since college. I try to stay away from junk food."

"Years? Everyone needs junk food once in a while, life is meant to be enjoyed. Don't you know that?"

I hadn't realized how snarky he was. McDonald's it was.

I backed out of the narrow parking spot.

"I don't even know where we can find a McDonald's around here," I said.

"Down the street, there's one on the corner of Dufferin and St. Clair," he said.

"Fine," I said, annoyed that I was taking direction from someone else.

We made the short drive to the McDonald's and I parked my car. There were homeless people standing outside asking for change. I noticed that Blue had stopped to fish some coins in his pocket and gave it to them before he caught up to me.

"Don't you need that money?" I asked him, thinking about how he'd been living on his brother's couch.

"I do." Blue shrugged. "But they looked like they needed it more than I do."

"I don't usually give homeless people money," I admitted. "They don't use it for good things, and then they never get a job because they know they can beg on the streets."

We waited in line. My dress shoes stuck to the floor and I realized that I was standing in what looked like spilled Pepsi.

"Do you know what you want to get?" Blue asked me.

I shrugged. "I think I'll just get a chicken salad...something that's not going to give me a heart attack."

He grinned. "That's boring, why don't you get a Big Mac, it won't kill you."

I shook my head, after seeing the calories displayed on the menu. It would completely kill all the work I'd been putting in at the gym.

We ordered our food and waited for our numbers to be called. I scanned the room, it was an unfamiliar feeling being in a place that I was so uncomfortable in. People stared at me because of how I was dressed, but also because of how uncomfortable I looked. I clearly didn't belong. I only entertained Blue's idea to come here because I wanted him to feel welcomed at my firm. More importantly, I wanted him to do a good job so that my company could continue to thrive and grow.

We finally received our food after waiting for a long time. It was different from the service that I usually received at the restaurants that I went to. The restaurant was full, and we couldn't find a seat anywhere. Finally, a booth next to the window opened up when a mom with her three kids left. We sat down and I used a napkin to wipe down the mess that the kids had left.

When we sat down, I realized that I was given crispy chicken instead of the grilled chicken I'd requested. I was going to head back to the counter and complain but I was already starving. I didn't want to wait another thirty minutes for them to make me a new salad.

Blue dunked some fries into ketchup and he took off the top bun off his burger to put the fries in it. I shook my head at how childish it was. But it made me smile at how happy a simple burger made him, while I was dissatisfied with my food that they had messed up.

Blue must have seen me pushing my salad around with a fork. "Try some of my burger," he said, offering his lunch to me.

It was a bit weird to be at a lunch meeting and eating my employee's food.

But I took a bite anyway and memories flooded back to my childhood when my mom had taken me there. Those memories were hazy, but the burger was as delicious as I remembered.

"See, it's good, right?" Blue asked.

I nodded. "It's not bad."

It was a new experience being here with Blue. I felt like I lacked power and control. If we were at a more upscale restaurant, one where the staff knew me, I'd feel more confident and at ease. But sitting here across from Blue, in a place where no one knew who I was, I felt like a nobody.

11

BLUE

I was confused. I knew it wasn't a date but it sure as hell felt like one. I wondered what Hunter's intentions were, and why he'd taken me out to lunch. Yes, he said he took all new hires out, but we hadn't even discussed anything business related yet.

It was funny to see him at a McDonald's because he looked so out of place. Even the way he was sitting looked uncomfortable. He had to tuck his arms in close just so he could fit his tall, muscular body in the seat.

"How's the job going so far?" Hunter asked.

The employees had gotten his order wrong, and he was picking off the crispy chicken off his salad.

"I don't know, it's hard to say. It just started, but so far everyone has been pretty nice," I said, taking a sip of root beer.

I didn't want to tell him the truth, which was that Marie, my supervisor, was being cold toward me. I didn't want Hunter to think that I couldn't handle the job.

"It's a good group of people, or I wouldn't have hired them," he said.

It made me feel better. Did he think I would be a good fit for his team? But my nerves kicked in again, that doubt in my head that said I'll be exposed as a fraud soon.

"How did you start your marketing firm?" I asked him.

He finished his bite before he answered, "I was young when I started it."

"And?" I asked, hoping to get more words out of him.

"I don't tell people this. But...I was homeless at the time, and I needed to find something I was good at so that I could get myself off the streets," he said.

I raised my brows, and I set my burger down on the tray. I tried to picture him homeless, but he was too handsome and put together. It made me see him in a new light. He was more human and knowing that he once struggled calmed my own nerves and self-doubt.

"Why were you homeless?" I asked him.

He glanced over his shoulders as if someone would hear us, but no one there was someone he'd run into.

"Gambling addiction," he said. "I got deep into blackjack, and it consumed every waking hour of my life."

"Did you stop eventually?" I asked.

"Yeah, I had to. I knew I had to channel my energy into something else more productive, so I went back to my passion which was marketing. It was hard at first. I went to job interviews, but because of how unkempt I looked, no one would give me the time of day. It was humiliating. I just wanted a job to get back on my feet, but there was no one who gave me a shot."

Suddenly, I realized why he'd hire me. I was him when he was younger. He saw something in me when no one else did. Hearing his pain and his struggle, and how he was opening up to me made me want to hold and touch him. It would be inappropriate since he was now my boss. But I couldn't help but be attracted to him. Even after he left Harry's apartment so abruptly the other night.

"So, you decided to start your own firm?" I asked. "Because no one gave you the chance?"

"Yes. I begged the bank to give me a small loan, but they saw my awful credit score and immediately disqualified me. I had to result to borrowing from high-interest lenders, so everything was on the line. Looking back, it was just another form of gambling. I was already in massive debt, and I was taking on more. I did all that for a dream that was in my head."

"And you made it," I said, smiling at him.

"I guess so, but I know the moment I stop working hard, I'll be back where I started. I can lose it all in a second," he said.

I was surprised that Hunter was telling me this because I barely knew him. Sure, I've seen him naked and showered with him, but it still felt like we were strangers.

"You've never told anyone your story?" I asked.

"Never," he said. "It's not like other people have to know, and they'll see me as less of a man if I tell them."

"I don't think so. I doubt anyone would think of you as less of a man for being honest. It's the truth, and you should embrace it," I said.

"People don't think like that—like you. They will pick the negative and spin it into their own story. I'd rather not have to deal with it."

What did he mean that people don't think like me? I knew I was just like everyone else. I wasn't special in any way. Most of my life, I'd tried my best to stay out of people's way because I was such a nuisance all the time.

We finished our food, and we left the McDonald's to go back to his car. The sun was beating down harder than it was all week, and even taking one step outside made me sweat like crazy. It didn't help that he had black leather seats, and it felt like sitting in a sauna when I climbed into his car.

Hunter got out of his parking spot but he couldn't get very far in post-lunchtime traffic. I wondered if we'd get back to the office any time soon.

We looked ahead and could see that there were people blocking the road, holding signs up. It was some kind of protest.

"Fuck, don't people have things to do rather than inconvenience people's days?" Hunter asked, slamming his palm on the side of the steering wheel.

"People have important messages that they want to share," I said.

"Well, my message to them is to get out of the way," he said, fisting the steering wheel even harder with his large hands.

It was the first time that I got a sense of his anger. He had a rough past.

I thought I had it bad after getting fired. But I could only imagine how devastating it was for Hunter to have once been homeless. I was fortunate enough to have a brother to turn to. He had to fend for himself and starting his own company from scratch.

Hunter was sitting in the driver's seat of his luxury car. His Rolex blinded me as it glistened and reflected the rays of the sun. These things were symbols that he made it despite the obstacles he faced. In my eyes, he had already proved himself. But I wondered if he thought it was enough.

We detoured to a side street to avoid the protest that had created all the traffic. We went down a residential road with mature trees on each side. Their branches reached out over the road, forming an arch that blocked the bright rays of the sun.

Kids were drawing on the sidewalks with chalk. They reminded me of the carefree summers in my childhood. There was little to worry about when I was younger. The only thing that was on my mind was hoping that it'd be sunny again the next day.

I was much bolder when I was younger. I remembered exploring unknown territories and being a fearless adventurer. I wondered where that boldness went.

"Why did you leave my place so abruptly?" I asked.

It was an attempt to be bold like I used to be.

The question must have startled Hunter. He twitched and jerked the steering wheel before he swerved back in line with the road.

"Don't talk about that night ever again," he said.

His voice was soft, but I knew how serious he was because of how quietly and slowly he'd said it.

"No," I fired back at him.

I knew what I said wasn't what he expected because this time, he stopped on the side of the road. We had passed the row houses and trees and were now facing a small park and an empty field.

"I mean it, Blue, I don't want to talk about that night."

"Why?" I asked him, pressing on. "Why can't we talk about it?"

"Because it was a mistake," he said.

His words cut me deep, and I was hoping that he wasn't going to say that.

"A mistake?" I repeated. "That's a lie and you know it."

Hunter was breathing heavily. his chest rose and fell rapidly, just like he had been right before he came in the shower.

"Tell me why you hired me if you thought it was a mistake," I said.

He was quiet, looking out ahead on the empty field.

"Because you reminded me of myself. Because I wanted to give you a chance. Not because I wanted there to be anything between us," he said.

I was nervous. I wasn't just talking to some guy who had rejected me. I was talking to the CEO of the top marketing firm in the country who had just hired me. There was more on the line than simply asking about a one-night stand. But it was important to me to get it off my chest if I was going to work for him.

"Look at me when you say that," I said. "Tell me you don't want there to be anything between us."

He turned to me and his brows furrowed. I could see the softness in his eyes. He didn't really mean it. I could tell that he was lying when he said he didn't want there to be anything between us.

I waited for Hunter to say something...anything. But he remained silent until he jerked forward so abruptly that I thought he was about to punch me in my face. But it wasn't a punch, it was a kiss. He pressed his lips firmly onto mine. It happened so quickly that my eyes were still opened for a few seconds before I knew what was happening. I closed them to take in his passionate kiss. His stubbled face pricked against my face, and the back of my head hit the passenger window. I reached forward to pull his body as close to me as I could. He'd unbuckled my seatbelt while still kissing me, and pulled me back toward him. His intoxicating scent and his cologne made my body weak.

My heart raced as his tongue entered my mouth, probing for my tongue. He groaned like a wild bear when he found it.

My hands moved down his thick torso, and I ran it against his hard-on before he pulled my face back to look me in my eyes.

"I left your brother's apartment that evening without saying goodbye because I was afraid that this would happen. I was afraid that I'd actually like you," he said.

His words stung my beating heart, and I opened my mouth to say something, but nothing came out. It was me who was speechless now. So instead, he kissed my pursed lips again. He pulled me onto his lap. Both my legs straddled the sides of his legs. My head grazed the top of his car. Hunter grabbed my ass, squeezing and kneading it with his large hands. My eyes opened when I heard the sound of something nearby. I realized that there was a mother pushing a stroller on the sidewalk. She was staring right at us. She took off her sunglasses so she could see if what she was seeing was really happening. When we'd stopped doing what we were doing to look back at her, she started walking as if nothing had happened.

"Oops," I said.

"I knew you were trouble," Hunter said, smirking.

When we realized that this was not the time and place to be on top of each other, I moved back over to my seat. Both of us straightened our shirts and ties as much as we could.

"We should really head back to the office, we're already very late," Hunter said, looking at the time.

I nodded and Hunter started the car again, heading back toward the office. It was past the lunch rush, so the streets were a lot quieter.

And though the feeling of kissing Hunter for the first time was so hot and passionate, I was left still wondering if there was anything more between us.

12

HUNTER

I didn't want anything to do with Blue because I was afraid of the very thing that became a reality.

I started having *feelings* for him.

That sentence made my skin crawl. There were rarely any feelings involved in business, and that was what I enjoyed the most about it. I didn't have to think about stupid things like my feelings. But Blue...Blue changed that after we shared that kiss, and I knew from that moment in the car, I wanted more.

I didn't want to talk about what happened that evening in his brother's apartment. But he made me talk about it. He made me tell him why I'd left, and it was because I liked it way too goddamn much.

We finally made it back into the office.

I let Blue enter into the office first so that no one would question why we'd been gone for almost three hours. I found a parking spot and straightened my suit before I walked back into the office. In the lobby, I saw Blue in the boardroom, standing by the door. Marie was sitting at the table opposite of where he was standing. Marie was speaking to him in an aggressive tone, her voice echoed in the lobby. Even the receptionist had turned her chair to see what was going on.

I walked toward Blue to see what was going on, and when Marie saw me, she immediately stopped talking.

"Is everything okay?" I asked, looking first at Marie, then at Blue. His cheeks were rosy and he looked embarrassed.

"I was letting him know that we do not tolerate three-hour lunches," Marie said. "Especially during summer, which is the busiest time of year."

I was afraid that that was what it was about.

"I'm sorry," Blue said, looking at Marie, with his shoulders slouched forward.

"Actually, it was my fault," I said. "We got caught up in our conversation, and I'd lost track of time. So, it's not Blue's fault."

Marie clicked the back of her pen on the table, her focus was still on Blue.

"Well, this project isn't going to finish itself," Marie said to Blue. "And you still have a lot to learn."

Blue nodded, looking down onto the floor.

"Why don't you head back up and continue," I said to Blue, putting my hand on his back. It was an excuse to touch him.

Blue looked at me and left the boardroom. I closed the door, with Marie still in the room.

"Listen," I said, sitting down on one of the dark green upholstered boardroom chairs. "I know you're concerned with what's going on with the company right now, and I appreciate that. But why don't you go a bit easier on Blue? It's his first day here."

"Go easier?" Marie asked, followed by a scoff. "Since when did we operate on being polite? Your motto has always been to get shit done no matter what it takes. What's gotten into you?"

I never let anyone speak to me like that. But I needed Marie in my company. She was my longest-standing employee, and I knew she deeply cared about my empire. Also, she was older and she reminded me of my mother. I had always been taught to respect my elders.

"Give him a chance, see what he's got in the tank, and let me know if anything goes wrong, I will deal with it myself," I said.

Marie clicked her pen again, and the sound was starting to irritate the fuck out of me. "Well, if any of our multimillion-dollar projects get ruined...it would probably be because of the kid."

I nodded. "Well, hopefully, it doesn't escalate to that. But again, I will deal with it if you have any problems with him."

I stood up and left the boardroom to go back up to my office. I knew I was protecting Blue. I was protecting him harder than I ever had with anyone in my life. Everyone had once been expendable to me.

I was putting my ten years of blood and sweat on the line for an inexperienced employee. Thinking about it like that made me second-guess every decision I'd made in the past week. That included the fact that I kissed him in the car just moments ago.

I knew I wasn't thinking straight.

When I returned to my desk, my focus was all off. The only thing on my mind was Blue's tender and pink beautiful lips. I so badly wanted to taste them once more. I wanted to taste him in the privacy of my own home. I wanted his lips to kiss every inch of my own body. I wanted his lusty eyes to lock onto mine and feel his quivering body against me as he did so.

I was worried about him more than anything. I was worried that he couldn't take the pressure of this industry. I was worried that I'd put him in a role that he couldn't do, that Marie could potentially tear him to pieces. But all I had to hold onto was trust. I trusted that things would work out in the end, and more than anything, the thing between us remained a secret.

I had already had to protect him once today. I didn't know if I could do it again before other people started to suspect something was going on between us. Especially with someone as smart as Marie, who'd helped me propel my company to where it was today. I knew that more than anything I had to be smart about it. I couldn't let my feelings for Blue—oh god that word again—get in the way of what I'd worked so hard to achieve.

It was a few days later when Blue knocked on my door. It was around lunchtime, and we'd done a great job of avoiding each other during work hours.

He was wearing a short-sleeved button-up, with black and gold stripes that ran vertically on it. The shirt showed off his tanned skin beautifully. His warm summer glow radiated my office, which in contrast, was plain and uninspiring.

"What's up?" I said, pointing at the door to remind him to close it.

He closed it gently and walked up to me instead of sitting on the chair across from my desk.

He leaned forward and kissed me on the lips just briefly, making me want more.

"You're trouble," I said, putting my index finger on the top of his neck and running it down to the first button on his shirt.

"You're the one who called me up here," he said, reminding me that I'd left a folded note and put it on his desk that morning.

"You're right," I said. "I was wondering if you were looking for an apartment."

"Yeah, I've been looking since the start of this week, but the rent in this city is ridiculous. I can't find anything in the city that's not over-the-top expensive or too far from the office."

"Does your brother mind that you're still on his couch?" I asked.

"He said no," Blue said, who came closer and sat on my lap. His ass pushed right against my cock that hardened immediately. "But I feel bad for staying there. It's not the biggest apartment, and I'm sure he'd like his own space back."

I smiled, running my hand up his shirt on the smooth valley of his back. He tilted his head back and leaned it on my shoulder.

"I missed you," he said, his voice was a quiet, lusting whisper for my affection.

"I missed you, too," I said, my lips were so close to his ear that I could feel the heat on the side of his neck. "I've been busy like I've always been. But don't think I forgot about you."

I didn't even have any time to sleep. So, I didn't get many chances to see Blue outside of work. There was the rare chance when I could sneak downstairs for an excuse to talk to him.

"I called you up here because one of the people in my network had a rental up for sale in the city. Are you interested in checking it out tonight?"

"Really? You did that for me?" he asked, turning around to straddle me in my chair and squeezing his hands on my shoulders.

"Well, it's not a big deal really. My friend was the one who helped me find my condo, so I asked him if he knew of anything for you."

I tried to downplay the fact that I was actively calling all my real estate friends. I was searching to see which one of my connections had something that was suitable for Blue. I knew how much it must suck to be sleeping on the couch every single night.

I could see that Blue didn't look as excited as I thought he'd be, and I wondered why.

"What's wrong?" I asked.

"Well," he said softly, moving his hands off my shoulders onto his own lap. "If they found your place, then the apartment that they've found for me is probably out of my price range."

"Don't worry, I asked if it was something affordable and he said yes. But either way, are you free tonight around seven? We can go check it out together."

He thought for a moment then smiled again. "If you'll be there, then seven is perfect."

I leaned in to kiss him on the lips that had a slight peppermint flavor to them. I took a deep breath, and the butterflies in my stomach reminded me of how wrong it was to be doing this during work hours.

"You better go," I said. "I'll meet you after work tonight."

Blue kissed me once more before he got up off my lap and left my office. All I could think about was how delicious his ass looked. I was hoping that this week, we'd get the chance to finally do more than kiss each other.

I had a meeting at my client's firm in the afternoon, it was an important one. One that I'd been preparing for all week. Marie was going to come with me to make the pitch, and it'd been a successful one.

The meeting had gone on longer than I expected, and when we were driving home in rush hour, there was a call. On my display, I saw it was someone from the office who was calling me, and I picked it up on Bluetooth while in traffic.

"Hello?" I said.

"Hey, it's me," Blue said, his voice played over my car's speakers, and Marie could hear everything.

I clutched the wheel harder, hoping he wouldn't say anything that'd let Marie know about our secret.

"I was wondering where you went? I didn't see your car outside. Did you tell me to meet in the back?"

"Yeah, I'll be right there. Listen, I have to go. Driving. Talk soon."

I hung up immediately and looked over at Marie, who had a raised brow and suspicious look on her face.

"What was that about?" Marie asked.

I pretended to play dumb. "What's what about?"

"Meeting out back," she said.

"Oh, umm," I stammered.

My brain was already fried after the three-hour meeting. "I was going to show Blue how to get in through the back door. Just in case he gets here before the receptionist in the mornings, or if he needs to get out after everyone leaves."

It was a flat-out lie that I came up with on the spot. It was better than saying nothing at all.

"You gave him a key to the back door? There are employees who've worked here for five years who still don't have a key."

"Well, I've noticed that Blue has been staying really late. So, I thought I'd do him a favor so that he won't have to worry about it."

I did have a spare key in my desk at my office, but it wasn't my plan to have given it to Blue. The lie was easier to tell than the truth, which was that I was helping him look for an apartment. That would've been much harder to explain.

Marie wasn't dumb. Though she'd nodded and hadn't asked any more questions, she seemed unconvinced. She furrowed her brows and her arms crossed, remaining silent for the rest of the trip back to the office.

13

BLUE

I was waiting in the back alley of the office just like Hunter had instructed. It was almost thirty minutes past when he'd asked me to be there, and I was wondering if he was even going to show up at all. It didn't help that the phone call was so short, and I wondered who he was in the car with that made him hang up immediately.

Just when I was about to head back to Harry's, I saw his car pull up the narrow road between the two brick buildings. I could finally breathe.

He drove up and stopped so that I could climb into the passenger seat.

"Sorry," he said, glancing to the side before he kissed me. "The meeting went longer than expected."

"I know you're busy," I said. "You don't have to apologize, but I'd appreciate it if you could just call if you're going to be late next time."

He moved his hand that was gripping his steering wheel and put it on my thigh, squeezing it firmly.

"I will next time. Marie was in the car, and I didn't want to say much. She's a very suspicious person, and I don't want there to be rumors in the office...for your sake since you just started."

I hated the secrecy between us. I hated how I couldn't openly hold his hand or kiss him whenever I saw him. That was all I wanted to do when I saw his handsome rugged face. I wanted his large hands to touch me and hold me in public. I was used to that with my ex-boyfriend. I'd already come out of the closet, and being with Hunter, it felt like I was being forced back into it.

We drove to meet Hunter's real estate friend. We arrived at a five-story apartment building. The building was located in Yorkville, the fashion district of the city.

"Hunter, you got to be kidding me. There's no way I could afford this place," I said, as he parked his car right in front of it.

There was a man in a suit that waved at Hunter, and I assumed that was his friend who was going to show it to us.

"Just wait until you see it," Hunter said, turning off his engine, and stepping out of the car.

I took a deep breath before I stepped out to join him.

"Blue, this is Greg," Hunter said. "He's been my friend for many years, and he's found both my office building and my condo. So, rest assured, you'll be in good hands."

Greg had the same dark-colored hair as Hunter except Greg had a hint of salt and pepper in both his hair and beard. They were similar in height as well. Greg was standing on the third step of the apartment building, making him even taller. So much so that I had to reach above my head to shake his hand.

"Wow, firm grip you got there," Greg said, he smiled and showed his teeth that were so white that I wondered if they were real. "We better get going, I have another appointment soon."

We went through the frosted double doors. The marble-tiled lobby had two elevators. I'd never lived in a place that had elevators, let along one that was this fancy. I felt my palms sweat. It was going to be awkward to let Greg and Hunter know that this was outside of my budget.

Greg and Hunter chatted and caught up as we waited for the elevator doors to open in the lobby.

We stepped into the cramped elevator and went up to the top

floor. When we stepped out, I noticed that there were more units than I thought there'd be for such a small building. Greg led us to the end of the hallway.

Greg opened the doors to the empty apartment. There were plastic sheets taped over the light hardwood. The apartment smelled freshly painted.

"Don't mind the mess," Greg said. "They've just finished renovating it today. Hunter called me just in time, right before they put an ad up to rent it out."

I stepped inside and the first thing I noticed was the beautiful view out onto the city. Below were people walking home from work. we were high up enough that the cars and pedestrians were not too noisy. But we were not too high that it made it feel like we were detached from the hustle and the action below.

"It's not too big," Greg said, stretching both his arms out. "But it's perfect for one person. The owners are looking for someone who's going to take care of the place, someone who's responsible. They're a retired couple, so they don't want to do too much work. They said rent is negotiable if I could find a person that matches what they are looking for."

Hunter had a smug look on his face with his arms crossed. It was like he knew that I was already falling in love with this apartment.

"What do you think?" Hunter asked.

I looked around, and I'd told myself that I wasn't going to make a rash decision. But I was already imagining how perfect it'd be for me. It was a studio apartment, so there weren't any bedrooms. But it was big enough that I'd be able to bring all my things from Harry's. There was a nook in the corner, facing the large windows that'd be perfect for setting up a small workspace. I could do my creative projects while looking out at the gorgeous view.

"This is perfect," I said, barely able to contain my excitement, I couldn't wipe the smile off my face.

"Yeah? Do you want to take it?" Greg asked.

I looked over at Hunter, who was leaning against one of the kitchen cabinets, and waiting for my response.

"Yeah, I am interested if we're able to negotiate the rent," I said.

"Perfect!" Greg said. "You saved me a lot of time, Blue. I'll let them know you want it. Since Hunter introduced you, I trust that you're the type of person that the landlords are looking for."

I smiled, but I felt an ache in my stomach when he said that. I didn't feel responsible. But for some reason, Hunter was pushing me into things that I'd never dream of ever doing or having. What if I wasn't fit for the job and he suddenly decided to fire me? What if he found out the fraud that I actually was. His idea of who I actually was as a person was completely flawed.

I wanted to take back the words I said. Suddenly I didn't feel so interested. But it was too late.

"I'll let you take a closer look," Greg said, looking at his watch. "I have another appointment to go to so when you're done, just lock the door and put the keys in Mailbox 506 in the lobby."

I shook Greg's hand and thanked him. Hunter did the same before he left and closed the front door of the apartment. It echoed in the empty space.

I was looking out at the gorgeous view when I felt Hunter's touch suddenly, and it'd made me jump.

"What do you think?" he asked.

I felt his face bury in my neck, as I looked out at the beautiful cityscape.

"It feels...like a dream," I said.

"I hope it's the most beautiful dream you've ever had," Hunter said.

His hand wrapped around my chest, as he kissed my left ear, making my cock harden up immediately.

I could already feel his erection on my ass, and it pulsed against my cheeks.

I didn't want to admit that I was scared, that this was all a mistake, that this was too much for me to handle. But with Hunter holding me and touching my body, he turned off the endless loop of anxious thoughts in my brain.

"I think this is perfect for someone like you," he said, trailing kisses down my neck.

He palmed my ass, squeezing it. "I have something in the car, stay right here," Hunter said.

He turned and disappeared through the front door, and I was left alone in the empty apartment.

I opened some of the cabinets in the kitchen, inspecting them. I turned the tap in the kitchen sink on and off. I went into the bathroom and touched the rugged stone texture of the tiles. Did I deserve such a beautiful apartment?

When I went back into the main space, Hunter had returned with a red gift bag in his hands. He handed it to me with that familiar smirk on his face.

"What is it?" I asked.

"Consider it your housewarming gift," he said.

I peeked inside and pulled out the bottle of red wine.

"I think we deserve to relax a bit, to celebrate your new apartment and your new job," he said.

I smiled. "Both of which you got for me," I said, reminding him.

"Hey, don't give me credit for everything. This is yours because you deserve it and I want you to engrave that fact in your mind. You deserve it."

Hunter reached into the bag to pull out a corkscrew which he used to open the wine, and he handed it to me for the first sip.

"I forgot glasses," he said.

I took a swig and handed it back to him, and he drank from the bottle as well. We sat down on a section of the apartment that wasn't covered with plastic sheets. We watched the sun set behind one of the tall glass buildings on the horizon. The setting sun was coming in through the windows so strong that I felt the warmth all over my body. I took in another sip of wine, feeling it course through my tense body and loosening me up just a bit. This apartment was going to take a bit of getting used to, but I was starting to feel more relaxed. I couldn't wait to tell Harry that I was finally moving out, I wondered what his reaction would be.

"There's one more thing in the bag," Hunter said, his smirk looked mischievous.

I cocked a brow at him and slid the bag closer to me to see what was inside. I pulled out a bottle of lube and a condom that was sitting in the bottom of the bag.

Hunter crawled forward and kissed me on the lips. His large body over mine cast a long shadow on the wall, and it made me realize how much bigger he was than me.

I leaned back taking his kiss until my back was against the hardwood floor.

"Do you want to?" he asked, with his nose touching mine.

"You want to fuck me?" I asked, my voice was shaking even after the wine.

"Only if you want me to," he said.

His hips moved forward thrusting them against mine. Our cocks pressed against each other.

The freshly painted white walls looked orange from the setting sun. The sun hit the side of his face, highlighting his sharp jawline.

I was scared that we were moving too quickly. I didn't want to get hurt again after getting out of a tumultuous relationship with my ex-boyfriend. That relationship was the reason that

I'd lost everything, including myself. It hit me that I was putting myself in the same situation all over again. If Hunter and I didn't work out, I knew that I'd lose my job and my new apartment. I looked into Hunter's strong gaze, and feeling his powerful energy. His racing heart beat against mine. How could I say no?

I could see how he was so convincing in the business world.

"Fuck me, Hunter," I said.

Hunter pressed his lips against mine. I reached to pull his pin-stripe suit jacket off his wide shoulders. He groaned as his lips locked onto mine, and our tongues swirled together.

Hunter reached down to unbutton my shirt. But he lost his patience and ripped it open instead, exposing my bare torso.

14

HUNTER

I knew I was good at sex, I knew the sex appeal I had, and what I was capable of. I knew how to make the other person want more of me. But it was different with Blue. Why was I so goddamn nervous? I could feel my heart beating halfway out my chest, and seeing his naked torso in front of me, made my palms sweat. I didn't know what to do with another man.

Blue reached for one of my hands, which was pressed against the hardwood floor. He pulled my hand toward his chest. I felt his hard pecs in my hand, squeezing and kneading it. I watched him moan and tilt his head back. I kissed his neck gently.

"This is incredible," Blue said, his voice lusting for my touch.

I kissed him lower on his body, first his collarbone, admiring the sparkle of light from the sun on his golden skin. He arched his back as I kissed him lower on his body until I had reached one of his nipples. I felt it harden against my tongue into a sharp peak. I looked up to see that he was biting his lips, clawing his hands against the floor.

I bit his nipple softly, feeling him squirm under the pressure of my body.

"Please," he said. "Don't stop."

I paused and could see the agony in his eyes. I smirked.

"I said don't stop," Blue said.

"I know, just want to tease you a bit," I said.

I had all the time in the world for him. Part of the reason why I'd gotten him this place was so that I could come by whenever I wanted. I wanted him all to myself. I knew that if he stayed at his brother's, I wouldn't have as many opportunities to come over and to fuck him.

Blue reached his hand on the back of my neck and tried to force me back down on his pink nipple which was still hardened. I remained rigid, letting him know that I was in charge, that I did what I wanted, and it wasn't going to change. Even considering how sexy he was.

He finally gave up, and I moved my body up to kiss him,

crushing the weight of my body onto his. I groaned at how toned his body was. It wasn't something I was used to, having slept with women my whole life. But I realized how I loved the firmness. I loved how I could leave my red handprints on him when I squeezed his pecs or his sides.

I turned him so that he was on top of me. Blue's ass pressed right onto my hard-on.

"Take my clothes off, baby," I said, looking up at him.

I gave him a bit of control now that I was the one under him. I wanted to see what he'd do to me.

He reached for my tie and pulled it toward him. He kissed me before he pulled it off my neck, tossing it across the floor. Then, slowly, he unbuttoned my shirt. He looked like he was about to open the best present that he was ever given. My body.

I was going to make sure that our first time was going to be unforgettable. I wasn't going to let him leave this apartment without remembering it for the rest of his life. I wanted him to think about me every waking hour of the day. I wanted him to call me in the middle of the night and ask if I could come over. Judging from his rounded blue eyes as he undid one button at a time, I knew he was already hooked.

He opened my shirt, revealing my torso, and he ran his hands along my furry chest. The heat of his hands felt good against my body, as Blue moved his ass forwards and backwards on my cock.

His hands moved down my abs and reached for my belt. He had a bit of trouble with my belt buckle, so I helped him out. I was so hard for him and I was excited to break free from the confines of my pants and my briefs. I closed my eyes waiting to be set free.

He unzipped me and then revealed my briefs before he stopped.

"What's wrong?" I asked, opening my eyes.

"No-nothing," he said.

But I knew what he was surprised about.

"Is it my briefs?" I asked.

He nodded. "Yeah, just wasn't expecting that."

"You mean how worn out they are?" I asked.

"Yeah, I didn't expect there to be..."

"Holes in my underwear?" I said, finishing his sentence.

He nodded.

"I hope you don't mind, I haven't changed my underwear in years. Even though I buy myself expensive suits and watches all the time, I refuse to buy new underwear. This pair, I've had with me for over ten years. Of course, I wash them after I wear them, but I'd never throw them away even though they're worn down."

"Why?" Blue asked. "I mean there's nothing wrong with it, but you can obviously afford to buy new pairs. Why don't you?"

"It reminds me of where I came from. I wear them underneath my expensive clothes so that I am reminded of how far I've come. It's the only way that I can remind myself daily that beneath the expensive facade, this is who I was."

Blue ran his hands over my briefs. The small holes in the worn-out spots revealed parts of my cock to him. I could tell how turned on he was. But his raised brows signaled his surprise that I haven't changed my underwear in over ten years.

He lowered his face onto my briefs.

My briefs stretched tight against my thighs because of how much I'd been working out over the years. He put his face on the side of my briefs, taking in my scent.

"Smells good?" I asked, putting my hands on the back of my head as a cushion against the hardwood.

"Smells incredible," he said. "It's so powerful, so...you."

I smiled. "I'm glad you like it."

His put his nose between my balls and my thigh, and he took in a greedy breath. I was loving how turned on he was.

His hand ran up to the elastic part of my briefs, which had worn down considerably. Small rips and tears were all over the band. The Fruit of the Loom lettering was faded and illegible.

He pulled them down just enough for my cock to pop out and he kissed my tip. The pre-come that had leaked from my horniness touched his lips, making them glossy.

He pulled my briefs back up, and then reached through the slit of my briefs to pull out my cock from there. He started sucking me, and I groaned in ecstasy. It was the first time another man had blown me.

"Wow," I said, over and over again. "It feels...so different."

He paused to smile at me. "It's better when a guy does it, am I right?"

"Yeah," I said, pushing his head back down to continue.

In one of the worn-out holes of my briefs, he reached to grab and squeeze my balls. The feeling was overpowering. I watched the tip of my cock disappear into his beautiful mouth. He slurped and sucked and licked me, but he couldn't get past halfway on my shaft. I was too big for him and I wondered if his ass was capable of taking my big cock.

My body was sweating all over, I peeled my unbuttoned shirt off my back. Blue's eyes remained closed, bobbing his head on my cock.

I squeezed him gently on his shoulders, and he looked up at me with my cock in his mouth.

"You're going to make me bust a load if you go on like this," I said.

"Do you want me to stop?" he asked.

"I want to fuck you," I said.

I sat up and leaned forward to kiss him. His lips didn't taste sweet anymore. There was a musky bitterness that I knew was from my own cock.

I unbuttoned his trousers and pushed him off of me so that he was the one lying down. I could feel his body tremble as I pulled them down slowly. He was wearing white underwear that hugged his bulge perfectly. Unlike mine, his underwear looked brand new. I ran my hands up the side, feeling the curves of his ass before I flipped him over. His slender and defined back muscles looked like a work of art, it was perfectly symmetrical. I ran my hands over it, down the small of his back, and pulled his briefs and his pants off of him. He was completely naked. My cock pulsed at the sight of his perfectly sculpted ass. I'd been curious about it ever since that night at his brother's apartment and now his ass was finally mine.

There was a small birthmark on his left ass cheek. At first, I ran my fingers over it, thinking it was a piece of lint. But realized that the small heart-shaped birthmark was part of him.

"You know about this?" I asked, kissing the mark gently.

"The birthmark?" he asked.

"Yeah," I said. "It's beautiful."

My kisses covered all over his ass that was covered with the finest blanket of blond hair.

I spread him open, exposing his tight pink hole to me for the first time. It was that moment when I realized that there was no turning back. Seeing his perfection in front of me, the beauty of the most intimate part of another man, I was hooked. I lost any control that I had left in me.

I lowered my face and buried it between his cheeks, tasting him for the first time. I flickered my tongue against his opening, feeling him tighten up. Blue moved his ass in circles as he got used to the pressure of my tongue.

I clawed onto his cheeks, spreading him open even further, and sticking my tongue deep inside him. Blue opened himself up to me.

"This tastes incredible," I said, groaning. "I can't believe I've never done this before with another man."

"It feels so good, Hunter. Please, don't stop."

He was making demands again. But this time, I didn't have any self-control to tease him. I buried my face even deeper inside him.

I felt a tingling sensation in my groin. I realized when I looked down that I was leaking pre-come all over the hardwood floors.

"I don't know if I can do this any longer," I said. "If I fuck you tonight, I won't last more than one second inside you."

I was being honest, and I knew that my first experience with him was going to be cut short at this rate. He was too sexy, and everything was too new to me. I knew my body, I had trained myself to have stamina. But Blue's sexiness had caught me by surprise.

Blue turned over and he sat up to kiss me. There was saliva all over my face from eating his ass so aggressively but he didn't seem to mind.

"We can save it for another night," he said.

I nodded. "I want our first time to be special."

I felt Blue's warm hand on my cock and he started stroking

me. In just a few strokes, I felt my muscles clench and tighten, then I released come all over Blue's chest. It dripped down the sides of his smooth torso, onto the hardwood floor of his new apartment.

"I'm going to come too," he said, stroking himself.

I leaned forward to kiss his quivering lips and felt his warm come against my body.

15

BLUE

I was nervous after he orgasmed. Last time, Hunter had run out, and I was worried that he was going to do the same. But instead, he had lain back down next to me, our sweat- and come-covered bodies against each other. I rested my head on his hairy pecs while he drew circles around my nipples with his fingers.

I could feel how hard he was breathing. Though we'd planned to fuck that evening, it was cut short because of how hot it was. Neither of us lasted long enough for it to continue. The condom and the lube were still sitting in the bag that Hunter had brought. It was next to the bottle of wine that was half empty. The orange sunset glow was gone and was replaced by the yellow city lights from the streets below.

Neither of us had the energy to go and turn on the lights or clean ourselves. So, we lay in each other's come- and sweat-covered bodies. I didn't want him to leave that night. But I knew that we weren't going to sleep on the hardwood floors. The apartment technically didn't belong to me yet. I didn't know when the painters or landlord were going to come back the next day to finish the renovations.

"How do you feel?" I asked.

"A bit numb now," Hunter said. "Trying to process what just happened."

His cock was still semi-hard when he tucked it back into the slit of his worn-out underwear. Seeing his briefs for the first time earlier had caught me by surprise. It had completely shocked me that he was wearing something like that. But at the same time, it was a turn-on because it wasn't what I was expecting. It made me realize that even though I thought I knew who Hunter was, I had no idea.

My curiosity about him grew stronger, and I wondered what else there was to uncover about him. What did his condo even look like? And what other secrets did he hold in his past?

I admired his confidence and that he'd worn his old pair of briefs even though he'd planned to fuck me that night. After all, he did plan ahead by buying wine, condoms, and lube. He had an attitude that screamed, *this is me, take it or leave it.*

I looked up at him, his dark brown eyes reflected the skyline.

"We should head home, it's getting late," he said.

Hearing him say that gave me flashbacks of him leaving Harry's apartment. My body felt cold all of a sudden.

"It's okay if you want to go," I said. "I understand."

I leaned forward to try and get up, but Hunter pulled me back toward him.

"I only say this because we both have work tomorrow. Not because I didn't enjoy what happened tonight," Hunter said.

I looked down at my vulnerable and naked body, feeling the need to cover myself up. I grabbed the closest thing, which was my pants that was on the ground next to us, and I covered my exposed cock.

"Will we...will we continue this?" I asked.

As soon as I said those words, I wanted to take them back. I didn't think I was ready to hear his answer.

"Yes, of course," Hunter said. "I won't leave you like I did last time. It was a mistake and I hope you know that. I didn't mean to just up and go without telling you. It's just that...I was scared of what might happen."

"Scared of what might happen?" I asked.

"Yeah, my biggest worry at the time was that I'd enjoy being with you...and it's already happened."

I looked up at him to see the small smile he had on.

"I like you a lot," Hunter said.

Just when I thought there were no more surprises that evening, Hunter had dropped a new one on me. I knew what he said and his words played endlessly in my head. Those words, I like you a lot, had once brought me joy, but now they scared the hell out of me after what happened with my ex.

"Did I say something wrong?" Hunter asked, breaking the silence in the room.

I shook my head and smiled tightly.

"I like you, too. But I need to be careful," I said.

"Careful of what?" he asked.

"I don't want to get hurt again."

I could feel Hunter's body tense up, his fists clenched next to his body. "Who hurt you in the past?"

"I dated someone for over five years. He called me his soulmate. But he had an addiction that ultimately caused us to separate. That's when everything went wrong. I started calling in sick to work all the time because I was devastated. Since he wasn't around to pay the bills, I was left with paying rent for an apartment I couldn't afford alone. And so, I was evicted and had to move in with Harry."

"That's horrible," Hunter said, his body relaxing just a bit. "But just know that situations like these are ones that make you stronger. So, learn from them, and know that if you survived that, then you can survive future obstacles."

I nodded, but there was still that churning feeling in my stomach. I wondered if Hunter meant what he said earlier.

His words played endlessly in my mind again.

I like you a lot. I like you a lot. I like you a lot.

I wondered how many people he'd loved in the past, and how many hearts he's broken.

"When you tell me, you like me a lot, do you mean it?" I asked.

"Of course, I never say things that I don't mean. I don't write checks that I can't cash," Hunter said.

I wanted to believe him, but my past relationship ruined my ability to trust anyone.

"Do you think you can promise me that you won't hurt me?" I asked.

I could feel his body shift further away from me. It was as if suddenly the room got colder and darker.

"I can't make that promise," he said.

Those words were my biggest fear.

"Why?" I asked.

"Because that's one thing that I'm not sure of," he said.

"What do you mean you're not sure?" I asked, confused more than ever.

I looked into his eyes. I still couldn't get over how sexy he looked, lying naked in the apartment that he'd found for me.

"Because that's something that I don't know. This is all so new to me. I don't know how to act or behave. In my business, I've learned that there are repercussions for overpromising. So, when you ask me if I'll ever hurt you, I honestly can't say yes or no."

What he said sounded reasonable, and it made me wonder if I was the one who was asking too much. I wasn't sure if my emotions were getting the best of me.

I wanted Hunter. Especially after what we just did together and how perfectly this evening had gone. I wasn't sure what to do or say. I didn't know if I should've ended things with him right then and there. I knew that if I continued to go down this path, things would turn out even worse than it did with my ex.

"Does that sound okay?" Hunter asked, his low voice hummed in a calming way that distracted my thoughts.

"I don't know. I think I need some time to think about it," I said.

"That's fair, we still have to be careful at work. This is still our secret, and we can't tell anyone about it."

There was that word again. Secret. I hated secrets. I wanted to throw up.

"I understand, but I don't agree with it," I said.

I bit my tongue to hold back what I really wanted to say, which was to tell him that I didn't want to be kept a secret.

"Okay, just know that we'll continue to have a great time together, and that's enough for me," he said.

"That's enough for you, but how about me?" I asked, challenging him again.

"Is this what you want? A relationship? You just told me that you got hurt by your ex. I don't think that you want to jump back into anything serious, and neither do I. So, what's the point?" Hunter said, not backing down.

He was as stubborn as I was.

I hated how convincing he was. It was hard to deny how head over heels I was for him, and I was thinking that he knew it as well. He had me wrapped around his finger. That feeling of having no control over anything has been something that I was used to my whole life. I hated that feeling, but it was all I knew.

I was too curious, too tempted by his mysterious demeanor, that I could just up and leave. Besides, he's already gotten me a job and an apartment. Could I really just leave that all behind?

"Okay," I said. "We'll just continue with the way things are without putting a label on anything if that's what you want."

His arms flexed as he leaned forward to bring his face close to mine. He kissed me gently.

"It's what I want," he said.

I rested my forehead against his and nodded.

"Why don't we shower off here, and I'll drive you back to your brother's so we can get a good night's rest," he said.

I nodded again.

We got up off the ground and used a rag that the painters had left to clean up the come stains off the hardwood. Then, we hopped into my new bathtub that didn't even have a shower curtain yet.

Our bodies pressed up against each other under the warm water. Hunter wrapped his arms around me, making me feel safe. He ran his hands over my abs and my pecs, washing away the sweat and come that he'd left on me. Then, he ran his hands between my ass cheeks.

Safe. A feeling that was good and bad at the same time. He had me feeling so safe that I wondered if it would turn out bad to feel too comfortable. I still had a chance to say no to this apartment that he'd gotten for me. Sure, sleeping on my brother Harry's couch was uncomfortable. But at least he was family. I could trust Harry. He couldn't kick me out unless I did something really, really stupid. But I knew Hunter had the power to take away anything he'd given me. Was I being paranoid because of what happened in the past? Or should it be something that I should genuinely feel nervous about?

There was a good reason for my paranoia. I had once thought my ex was perfect, but I realized quickly that no one was. And the scary thing was that Hunter's flaws weren't easy to find. He did a great job of hiding them if he had any flaws.

"Fuck," Hunter said, water dripping down his body. "We don't have any towels."

Neither of us thought about that before jumping into the shower.

"I guess we're going to have to air dry," I said, smiling.

Hunter turned off the water, and he used his big hands as a kind of squeegee to wipe away some of the water off my body.

"It's alright, the heat outside is going to dry us off quickly anyway."

I used my hands to dry him off as well. Running my hands all over his body made me hard again, and I could see that he was too. Hunter stepped out first, putting his briefs back on, which now had a few stains on them next to the worn-out holes. It was a turn-on to see that he wasn't all perfection. It made him a bit more human. Funny enough, his old underwear was sexier to me than the expensive clothes that he put over it.

We got dressed and locked the front door of my new apartment. We went back downstairs and returned the key in the mailbox like Greg had instructed us to do.

16

HUNTER

It was a week later when Blue called to let me know that his apartment was ready for him to move in. I had pressured Greg to tell the landlords to give him a good price because Blue was reliable. I knew that he'd take care of the place.

I offered to help Blue move. It was a Saturday, sunny, and I could use a bit of sun for my tan and a little workout from lifting heavy things. Plus, I knew that Blue didn't have very many things and that it wouldn't take up too much of my day. It was the first weekend I had where I didn't feel completely swamped by work. It would also be nice to spend a bit of time with Blue.

I arrived at his brother's apartment. It was the first time I'd been there since that evening. I called, and Blue came downstairs to let me in. Sweat glistened on his skin. I could tell from the smile on his face that he either was excited to see me or excited to move out. Maybe both. I was glad that I got to see him on that day because I knew it was a huge leap from his current situation.

When we got inside the lobby, and I was sure that there was no one there, I grabbed Blue's face and kissed him against the wall.

"Missed you," I said.

He smiled and it had a contagious effect on me.

"You miss me? I saw you just yesterday at work," he said.

"For like five seconds before we were interrupted by Marie," I said.

"I think she likes you."

"What?" I asked, scratching my head. "She's old enough to be my mother."

"Right, there's a word for that, it's called being a cougar."

I smiled. "I already have a little lion here, I don't need a cougar," I said, putting my hands on his ass and squeezing it. The door swung open and an older man who lived there saw us all over each other. I cleared my throat and backed up off of Blue, moving to the side to let him cross. I felt uncomfortable, even though I didn't know the gentleman. The fact that he saw us touching each other worried me, and I couldn't wipe that concern out of my mind.

"Where's all your stuff?" I asked Blue, as we made our way upstairs to his brother's unit.

"A lot of it is already in the truck. But there are a few boxes left that are pretty heavy, so it'll be perfect for you to lift," he said, squeezing my bicep gently.

I smiled and we walked into the apartment. I was surprised to see Blue's brother on the couch, watching what sounded like the soccer game. It was the first time that I saw him sober. He stood up to greet me. Though his face resembled a bit of Blue's face, his skin was much paler, and of course, he had red hair instead of blond. He was much taller than Blue but not as tall as me.

"Hey, I'm Harry. You must be Hunter," he said, reaching his hand out to shake mine.

"Pleasure," I said, shaking his hand.

Though he'd come to greet me, his presence wasn't too friendly. He pulled my hand toward him aggressively when he shook my hand. I wondered if he wanted to fight me.

"I've heard some things about you from my brother Blue," Harry said.

I smirked. "Only good things, I hope."

Blue and I had never discussed anything about his brother. But I was hoping that Blue had kept the secret between us. I didn't know how close he was to Harry. Judging from the fact that Harry had offered his place to Blue, I had a feeling that they were pretty close.

"Of course, good things. I don't let my brother hang out with anyone who's not good for him," Harry said.

We were still shaking each other's hands and staring each other down. Neither of us was going to let go.

"Can one of you strong men help me with this box?" Blue asked. It was good timing because both of us weren't going to back down any time soon. I wondered what Harry's problem was.

"I will," I said, helping Blue carry the box.

Blue and I walked downstairs to the truck that was parked on the side of the road. It was a small U-Haul cargo van. His belongings barely even filled up half the van.

"What did you tell your brother about me?" I asked, sliding the box into the bed of the van.

The contents inside rattled and it sounded like there were plates inside.

"Nothing," Blue said, looking at me with his crystal eyes.

"Really? He seemed a bit...aggressive."

"He's like that," Blue said, scratching the back of his neck and making me lust over his beautiful toned arm. "Don't take it personally, he's just trying to look out for me."

"Alright," I said. "He should be grateful that I carried his drunk ass home instead of trying to intimidate me with a handshake."

"You talked to him for two minutes just now. You're already butting heads?"

"I'm just trying to figure out what his deal is. I'm not here to fight him or anything, but he should learn to be careful when he's pulling these alpha male moves on me."

"You guys are so similar. I don't understand why men have to one-up each other like that," Blue said, smirking.

I climbed down from the bed of the truck, and Blue closed the door behind me.

"Just try to get along, will you?" Blue asked.

I nodded reluctantly.

I sat in the U-Haul next to Blue and Harry. Harry was driving, and Blue sat between us. I wasn't used to not being in the driver's seat. It didn't help that Harry's driving was giving me a bit of anxiety from how fast he was going.

Blue held his hands in his lap. Since Harry and I were so big, Blue had to round his shoulders forward so that we could all fit in the front.

"So, what do you do?" Harry asked.

"I'm the CEO of Magna Marketing," I said, holding onto the side of the van as Harry turned aggressively. There were boxes in the back that sounded like they'd fallen over because he was going so fast.

"CEO..." Harry said. "I see."

He was a mix between passive-aggressive and straight-up aggressive. I was wondering why. I was the one who'd helped him home that night, but he wouldn't have remembered it unless Blue had told him.

"What do you do?" I asked him.

"I'm in construction," he said.

"I could have guessed that," I said.

"What is that supposed to mean?" Harry asked.

I didn't like his tone.

"Well, just from your steel-toed boots," I said, pointing down to his shoes.

I didn't want to start a fight with him in front of Blue, though I was more than capable of taking him on if he made the first move.

"I'm wondering why my brother's boss is helping him move," Harry asked.

"Cut it out," Blue said, nudging his brother on the arm. "You're asking too many questions."

"I'm not his boss, technically," I said. "And I just want him to know that I'm here to support him because I see potential in him."

I rolled down the window to bring in some fresh air, and to cut some of the tension in the cramped van. I wasn't there for Harry, I reminded myself that. I was there to help Blue, and I wasn't going to let his brother think that he could intimidate me.

We finally arrived at Blue's new apartment, and we got out of the U-Haul and brought the boxes onto the yard in front. Blue had a huge smile on his face. I was glad to see how much higher he held his head that day, and how proud he seemed of his new apartment.

It reminded me of the time when I found an affordable apartment after getting off the streets. Knowing that I could shower every day, and knowing I had my own bed to sleep in meant everything to me at the time.

Blue and I brought the boxes upstairs while Harry stayed outside to keep an eye on the van.

Blue and I moved as many boxes as we could into the elevator. We had to stack them high, but we left enough room for the both of us to fit inside. It was tight in there, as we went up to the fifth floor. Our bodies were pressed up against each other in the midst of all the boxes. I could finally kiss him in privacy. His lips were sweet as always, and I put a finger on his chin to bring his face up to meet mine.

"Don't mind Harry today," Blue said, resting his chin on my shoulder as I embraced him.

"What's his deal? I don't know why he's being so aggressive," I said.

"He's just looking out for me because he knows what happened with my ex in the past. He gets extra protective of me whenever I meet someone new in my life. I'm glad you came today. Harry's a great brother, but he's lazy when it comes to actually doing things."

"Not a problem at all," I said, kissing him again. "I actually enjoy moving, unlike a lot of people."

"You do? That's kind of weird. I don't think I know anyone who enjoys moving."

"Well, I guess it's because I'm good at organizing, and making things efficient. So, I know how to move effectively," I said.

"Well, if anyone I know wants some help moving, I know who to call," Blue said, followed by a laugh.

"You're a joker. I don't have time to just help any random stranger to move. I'm only doing this because—" I cut myself off when I realized what I was about to say.

"Because of what?" Blue asked, pushing his body closer to mine, sandwiching me between him and all the boxes.

"Because I like you," I said.

He smiled. "Well, I like you too."

I admired how simply he could say those words, whereas I felt so uncomfortable saying it.

I wished that the elevator ride lasted longer. When the metal doors opened, both of us sighed. We knew that we had to move the boxes quickly before the elevator door made that annoying buzzing sound. We slid the boxes, moving them one at a time until we finally got them all out in the hallway.

Then, we walked into Blue's new apartment. The walls had a

fresh coat of paint, and all the tarps had been removed as well.

"Welcome to my home," Blue said.

"It suits you," I said.

He smiled. "I can't wait to get a bed."

I raised a brow at him and seeing his dimples had me smiling as well.

"What are you going to do on it?" I asked.

"Just sleep," he said, giving me a wink.

"Just sleep, I see. Nothing else?"

"No, just going to use that bed for resting."

"We'll see about that," I said, winking back at him. "You better make sure that bed can handle a lot of force," I said, biting my bottom lip.

"Why? It's not like I'm going to be jumping on it or anything."

"There won't be any jumping, but I'll assure you that there will be lots of intense, sweaty, passionate fucks."

I could already feel my cock harden at the thought of it.

17

BLUE

All my muscles were sore from moving. It was Monday morning, the worst day of the week. I turned off the alarm which was blaring a classic Fleetwood Mac song. I'd once really enjoyed that song but now hated it because it reminded me of getting out of bed.

I was sleeping on some bubble wrap that was left over from the move. My back ached. It may have been better if I had just slept on the hardwood. I couldn't wait for the bed that I ordered to arrive.

I got ready and made some instant coffee, which was the only thing in my cupboards at the moment, and I made my way to work.

The office was a lot closer than it was before. My commute

took half the time it did when I lived at Harry's so I arrived earlier than expected.

I set my backpack down and noticed there was a note on my desk, and I was curious to see who'd left it.

I opened it up, and read it.

> *Please see me ASAP when you arrive this*
> *morning.*
> *- Marie*

There were a few pen marks beneath where she signed her name. I knew it was from her clicking her pen, I could practically hear the sound in my head. It had always made me a bit nervous when she was walking down the hallway making that sound with her pen. She was my supervisor so I had to report to her. But ever since meeting her at the interview, she'd never seemed to like me or even want to get to know me. The only time she ever talked to me was to give me things to do or tell me what I did wrong.

I delayed going into her office as long as possible. I went to hide in the kitchen to wash my travel mug. In there, I did some breathing exercises I'd learned from yoga when I used to go regularly.

I finally mustered up the courage to go see her.

Her office door was left ajar, and I could hear her typing something on the computer. As always, when I walked in, she refused to acknowledge me first.

"Hi, Marie," I said, with a tight smile.

My palms started sweating as soon as I walked into her office. It was like I was the dog in Pavlov's experiment, waiting for my electric shock.

"Sit down," she said.

I listened and waiting until she finished what she was doing.

She had the second largest office in the firm besides Hunter's. Marie always wore black and she had many variations of black dresses. This one had long sleeves and a wide neckline that exposed the sunspots on her collarbone. She didn't have a ring on her finger, so I assumed she wasn't married. But she'd often walk around the office talking to people about wanting a baby.

"Do you know why I called you in here?" she asked.

Marie always asked me this and I never knew why. I thought long and hard. After a tiring weekend of moving, I couldn't even remember what I had for lunch yesterday.

I shook my head.

"Do you know anything around here?" she asked, followed by a scoff. Before I could even answer, she started talking again.

"Look at these documents that you were in charge of and tell me what's wrong," Marie said.

She slammed the stack of papers in front of me, and it'd made me jump a bit in my seat. I tried to remain calm and cool, but it was very difficult around Marie. I'd never been especially good at talking to authority figures. Marie was definitely not helping with it.

I sifted through the sheets, trying to see if I noticed anything wrong. Looking through them, I realized that I had never submitted them because I wasn't finished yet.

"I am still working on these," I said.

"Right, and when will you have them to me by?" she asked.

Her tone was so loud and aggressive that I was sure other employees in the office could hear her. Blood rushed to my cheeks.

"You said Friday, so I was hoping to get it to you before the end of this week," I said.

"End of this week," Marie repeated, the veins in her neck were becoming more and more visible. "I said Friday, as in last Friday."

"That's impossible," I said, trying to defend myself. "You only gave me this assignment on Thursday. There was no way I could've completed it in one day."

"Then you should've made it clear to me, and you should've been working on it this weekend. I am very disappointed in your performance at this job so far...it wasn't like I had high hopes to begin with."

Her words jabbed me right in my stomach and I tried my hardest not to break down into tears. She wasn't being fair. She knew it and I knew it. But there was nothing I could say or do to change that.

"I'm sorry," I said. "I'll try to do better next time."

"I'm afraid I'm going to have to talk to Hunter about this. He'll be very disappointed as well."

"No, please. Give me a chance. I'll finish them by tomorrow, even if I have to stay here all night."

"The client is already angry at us. Hunter will know about it even if I don't tell him."

"Why wasn't I given this assignment earlier if it was so important? I had no idea that the deadline was one day to complete an entire package. There's no way I can work that fast yet. I just started working here."

"Well, you should've thought about what you're capable of

before accepting this job."

I shook my head in disbelief. I couldn't even look at her eyes. She was staring right at me, trying to break me.

"You may leave my office now," Marie said.

"Is there anything I can do to fix this before Hunter finds out?" I asked.

I didn't want it to get to that point but I was willing to beg if I had to. I couldn't lose my job and I couldn't let Hunter find out that I wasn't capable...that I was a fraud. I was hoping that I could prove myself wrong in this job. I knew Hunter would be disappointed if he found out.

"There's nothing. Now leave, please. Unlike some people, I actually have things to do."

Marie pulled out her pen from her desk and starting writing notes onto a notebook.

I lowered my head and left her office. Eyes followed me when I walked back to my desk. People had definitely heard the entire conversation. I felt like garbage. I went back to my desk and I wasn't sure what to do. Was it too late to continue the work that was apparently already overdue? I felt utterly defeated. I wished that I could turn to Hunter, who was just two floors up, to ask for help. But I didn't want to disappoint him, and I didn't want to be the one to break the news that I fucked up.

I sat at my desk, frozen still, hoping no one would notice me. I hoped that people would forget what they heard in Marie's office sooner rather than later.

I waited for Marie to give me some kind of direction, but she wasn't going to give me anything. Her office was directly in line with where I was sitting and she could see my every move. I felt like her prey, helplessly waiting for her to eat me alive. I knew I wasn't cut out for this job. I wished that I never accepted it in the first place so that I wouldn't have to disappoint Hunter.

After lunchtime, I noticed that Marie wasn't in her office. My only guess was that she was upstairs talking to Hunter, letting him know all the reasons why I should be fired. How could I defend myself if she was talking behind my back? I hated office politics. I wished that I could just do my work without worrying about being on Marie's good side. But I knew that this was part of the deal.

Time passed slowly and I periodically wiped my sweaty palms on my trousers. I rehearsed lines in my head of what I was going to say during the meeting with Hunter and Marie. I even tried to mentally prepare myself for getting fired.

Who cares anyway? I had already been fired recently.

Getting fired a second time was no big deal. I'd lose my apartment. There was no way I could afford it without my job. I'd have to move back to Harry's place though. I sighed, thinking about how I'd just gotten used to the beautiful, new apartment. I had already made plans to decorate to make it my own.

I put my hands over my eyes, wishing that I called in sick that day. The churning feeling in my stomach was starting to feel unbearable.

"Blue," Marie called from the direction of the elevator. "Come now."

I had no choice but to follow her. My life depended on it. The ride down to the lobby was awkward. I figured I was going down so that she could escort me out of the building. Marie didn't crack a smile, let alone look at me. It felt like I was descending down to the gates of Hell.

I was surprised when she took me into the boardroom instead of being escorted out. Hunter was sitting down at the head of the table. He looked handsome as ever and freshly shaved that day. I couldn't help but smile when I saw him. I wondered what important things he had that day that had him looking so dapper. But he always looked good no matter what.

Marie slammed the door behind me.

I sat down in one of the chairs across from Hunter. I was always a bit nervous around him. I still couldn't really figure him out entirely. With Marie in the room, my trembling was even more apparent.

There were a few minutes of silence. Hunter was finishing up an email on his laptop before he closed it and focused his attention toward us.

I swallowed the lump in my throat, preparing for the news that they had to fire me.

"So, I was made aware that there are some problems about work not being completed on time," Hunter said calmly. "I want to get the story straight and make sure I'm hearing both sides. Blue, why don't you explain what's been going on?"

I wasn't expecting the opportunity to tell my side of the story. But Hunter was being fair and giving me the chance to do so.

"I wasn't aw-aware that the dead-deadline for this project was la-last Friday," I said. "I would've made it a pri-priority had I known."

It was hard for me to form a sentence together with Hunter and Marie in front of me. Marie tapped her pen against the table while I was talking.

Marie shook her head and she was itching for her opportunity to speak.

"I see," Hunter said. "Seems like there's a bit of miscommunication between the both of you."

"There are absolutely no communication errors," Marie said. "I've had over twenty years of experience managing and delegating tasks. If there are any errors, it's pretty obvious who's making them."

I remained silent. Saying anything at all was only going to further dig my own grave.

18

HUNTER

I wasn't going to lie, it was a bit endearing to see Blue so shaken up by what was happening. It showed that he really cared about the job. I wanted to tell him that it wasn't as serious as Marie made it out to be. But I knew I couldn't tell him or protect him in front of her. I knew how she worked. Her style was to get shit done no matter what.

"Look," I said. "How about this. From now on, let's have deadlines written on a calendar. That way, it's not easily miscommunicated. How does that sound?"

Blue nodded. I could see his body loosen up when I said that. But Marie didn't look happy about it. I didn't know why she disliked Blue so much. After hearing her rant about him, I worried about my decision to hire Blue under her supervision.

"I won't tolerate any more errors," Marie said. "It's already been weeks of hell trying to get Blue organized, and so far, it's not getting anywhere—"

"He'll get there eventually," I interrupted. "Let's work together here, we're all in this together. Blue, you may go back to your desk."

He lowered his head and got up to leave the boardroom, closing the door behind him.

"I don't know what you see in him, but it's starting to scare me," Marie said.

I furrowed my brows.

"What is that supposed to mean?" I asked.

"You would've handled the situation completely differently if it were someone else. You wouldn't let someone get away with such a costly mistake that easily."

I wondered if she was right. Were my feelings for Blue messing up my own business? I tried to think what I would've done if it was somebody else. I'd surely have taken Marie's side. If she'd ask to fire someone who wasn't Blue, I would've listened to her. Marie was one of my most trusted advisors and she's contributed to the success of my firm.

"Well, let's just see what happens. If there are any problems, bring them to me before it's too late," I said.

Marie wasn't going to willingly accept my response. But even she knew that my decision was final.

Marie left the boardroom, and I remained there to finish up some emails. I tried to stay focused, but the whole time I was thinking about Blue. I hoped that he was doing alright and hanging in there. It wasn't an easy job, and I hoped that he at least knew how to swim after getting thrown into the shark tank. I knew what Marie was capable of. She wasn't a nice person. But she was a vital part of my business. Without her, things would go haywire. I hoped that she'd give Blue at least a chance to redeem and prove himself. I just knew that there was more in him.

It was dark by the time I was ready to leave the office. When the elevator doors opened, I noticed that one of the lamps were still turned on in an otherwise dark room. I was surprised to see Blue working away. His face glowed blue from the computer screen.

"Burning the midnight oil?" I said, walking toward him.

He turned around, jerking back in his chair.

"You scared me," he said.

I went up to him and squeezed his shoulders.

"I hope you're not trying to take my job," I said.

"What? Why would you say that?" he asked.

"Because I'm usually the last one here. What in the world are you still doing here?"

"I'm trying to finish the project that Marie got mad about. I want to finish it by tonight. I think that'd make her happy."

I smiled at his dedication.

"Good luck," I said. "There's nothing that makes Marie happy."

He sighed, throwing his arms back behind his head and swiveled his chair around to face me. I leaned against the desk opposite of him, admiring how cute he looked that day. He wore a black dress shirt with his sleeves rolled up and showed off his tanned and toned arms.

"You hungry?" I asked, looking down at my watch. "It's been a while since lunchtime."

"I haven't even had lunch," he said, clutching both his hands on his stomach. "I didn't have time to prepare something after moving this weekend."

Poor thing must've been so exhausted.

"How about we grab something to eat? I'll buy. Then you can come back here if you want. But you should really go home after. What you're working on is honestly not as important as Marie made it out to be."

"I want to finish, Hunter. I don't want her to be disappointed anymore."

I nodded, "Okay, if you say so."

His eyes moved down my body and he had a mischievous grin on his face.

"What?" I asked.

He pointed down to my pants and I hadn't realized that I was bulging in my trousers. I was hard from just looking at him.

"You're horny," he said.

"You can say that again. It's been a while since I got to do things with you and you still owe me that thing you promised."

"What thing?"

"Your ass and letting me fuck you."

I could see his cock grow in his trousers too.

I looked around the office to make sure there was absolutely no one left. It was dead silent.

"I don't remember promising you that," he said. "But I can certainly spare a few moments to make sure you leave the office happy today."

I smiled.

"You want to do it here?" I asked.

"Well, I was going to suggest going back to your place or mine. But probably better if it was yours because you actually have a bed and I've never seen it before."

I thought for a moment, then smiled.

"Would you be opposed to fucking at the office, right here, right now?"

I could tell from his smirk that he wanted it as bad as me, especially after having such a stressful day.

"Not opposed to it at all. You're the CEO, which means you have to make the executive decision," he said.

I smiled and walked over to kiss his lips. He tilted his face to meet mine, and he parted his lips to take my tongue in.

"Wait here," I said, breaking the kiss.

"Where are you going?" he asked, his voice was needy.

"Just wait here," I repeated.

I ran to the elevator awkwardly because of my raging hard-on and went to my car which was parked on the street. I'd kept the bag with the condom and lube in my trunk. It was the housewarming gift that Blue and I didn't get to use last time. I rushed back into the office to Blue.

He saw what was in my hand and immediately remembered what was inside. It wasn't ideal that we were in my office, but it was hard to control myself at that moment. Seeing Blue after a long day was exactly what I needed. The thought of making love to him in my office was so taboo it made it that much hotter.

I walked up slowly toward Blue, who was sitting in his chair. His face was eye level to my cock, and he looked up at me with his lusty eyes.

"You sure?" he asked.

I nodded, giving him permission. He slowly undid my belt, teasing me, before thumbing open my button, and unzipping my trousers.

I was wearing a worn-out pair of boxers, and as soon as Blue saw them, he buried his face into them, taking in my scent.

My groan echoed in the dark and quiet office. I loved how turned on Blue was by my old boxers. These ones were red, but they'd faded so much in the wash over the years that they were almost a salmon color. Small holes covered every inch of them. A large rip was torn in the side next to my balls from the days when I used to play rugby in high school.

Blue reached through the rip and grabbed onto my cock. I groaned out loud, feeling his warm hands stroke me. He took my cock into his mouth.

"Baby boy," I groaned, marveling at how good it felt.

Blue swirled his tongue around the tip many times, and the sensation was overwhelming. I was once again caught off guard at how different it felt to be sucked off by another man. It only made sense that it was better, because after all, Blue was a man, so he'd know what did and didn't feel good.

I grabbed onto the back of his head, pushing him deeper down my shaft until I felt myself hit the back of his throat. Blue looked up at me, my cock in his mouth.

I groaned and nodded to give him approval that he was doing a good job.

I pulled my hips back and took my cock out of his mouth, then I grabbed Blue under his arms and lifted him up onto the desk.

"Are you sure this is okay?" Blue asked, looking around the office.

"I don't have a choice now, there's no way I'm going to stop," I groaned in the heat of the moment.

"Yes, boss," he said.

Blue calling me his boss turned me on. It made me feel powerful.

I undid his pants as quickly as I could, as Blue kicked off his dress shoes. I pulled his underwear off and tossed it on the ground. I ran my hands over his legs, admiring how toned they were. His cock twitched when I squeezed his thighs. I kissed him, pressing his head against the cubicle divider, Blue reached for my cock and stroked me. I groaned in his lips and he moaned back to me.

"You're going to have to help me out here," I said, ripping open the condom wrapper and putting it on my cock. "This is my first time with a man."

"Go slow," Blue said, opening the bottle of lube and squeezing it on the top of my shaft, then rubbing some onto his hole. He spread himself open to me, pressing his thighs to his chest and I admired how beautiful his pink hole looked. I undid the buttons on my shirt, and Blue ran one of his hands on my hairy torso.

"Slowly," he said.

I nodded and aimed my cock into his hole. I had no idea how he was going to take me. I didn't want to hurt him with my thick cock. I pushed into him, slowly. The lamp lit up the side of his face. He shut his eyes and he had a pained expression on his face.

I felt my cock squeeze into his tight hole. I groaned at how amazing it felt to be inside another man for the first time. I couldn't believe that I'd never done something that felt so good before. I inched inside slower, the further I got, the tighter he felt, but Blue took me like a champion. I grabbed his hips and kissed him, before thrusting my whole cock in, and Blue cried out in pain and pleasure. I leaned over him and kissed him as I drove my hips in and out of him.

"You're so fucking sexy," I groaned in between kisses.

"Don't stop," he said. "Please, don't stop."

"I won't, baby," I said, fucking him harder.

His moans made me fuck him harder and faster. I worried that the table wasn't going to support the force of my body slamming into him.

Sweat dripped down my forehead onto his body and his desk. I could feel my muscles tense up in anticipation for an orgasm.

"You're going to make me come, Blue," I said, driving my cock deep inside of him.

Blue started to stroke himself, and he put his other hand behind my neck, bringing me in for a kiss.

"Do it, boss. Let's come at the same time," he moaned.

I nodded, and a few moments after, I erupted in a mind-numbing orgasm. I felt Blue's warm semen cover my abs and on her chest.

We breathed heavily together, our noses touched, and I looked into his eyes.

"You're bad," I said, smirking.

"Hey, it was your idea," he said.

"Still, you made me do it."

I pulled my cock out of him by the base of the come-filled condom. As I gave Blue one last kiss, I heard the familiar sounds of the rusty elevator gears. Both Blue and I looked at each other in shock. There was still someone in the office.

19

BLUE

I could see the panic in Hunter's eyes as he scrambled to put his pants back on. I heard the elevator door open as I got off my desk and palmed the floor for my shirt. There was the clicking of heels down the hallway. We both stared in the direction of where the footsteps were coming from. Hunter backed away from me, scrambling to tuck his shirt back in his pants. I scrambled to put my clothes back on.

It was Marie who'd come back into the office.

"Oh," she said, pausing and looking us up and down.

My cheeks turned hotter than they already were after getting fucked by Hunter. There was the undeniable scent of sweat and sex in the air. Hunter and I both froze in silence.

"You're still in the office?" Hunter asked, his voice was shakier than ever before.

"I came back for my house keys," Marie said, looking down at her watch. "Am I...interrupting something?"

When she said that, I knew she was aware of what we did. Marie wasn't stupid. We had disheveled hair, sweat that dripping down our necks, and the room smelled of sex.

"Of course not," Hunter said.

I turned to sit back down and faced my screen. I wanted to run out of there, but I froze instead. My sticky lube-covered fingers touched the keyboard. My heart was beating faster now than it was when Hunter was fucking me.

Marie walked between us to get to her office. I noticed that the ripped-open condom wrapper was by my feet. I quickly put my foot over it so that Marie couldn't see it.

As she walked by, she smelled of alcohol. I suspected that she'd went for drinks after work and had come back to get her things before going home. I should have known that she was coming back. Her coat was still hanging by her door, and her laptop that she always took with her was still sitting on her desk.

"You know there are lights in here," Marie said over my shoulder. "You don't have to work in the dark."

"I know," I said. "I was about to leave, but I just wanted to finish this last thing for you."

"You sure you don't want me to turn it on?" Marie asked again.

"Don't worry about it," I said, not wanting her to see more than she already did.

She knew exactly what was going on between Hunter and me. I was sure of it, and I so badly wanted to disappear. The embarrassment was too much for me to handle. Marie went into her office and turned on the light in her office. The rectangular beam of light hit Hunter and me like we were suspects in an interrogation room. As Marie went to collect her belongings, Hunter ironed out his shirt on his body with his hands. He fingered his hair to comb it properly. I picked up the condom wrapper on the floor with a tissue and tossed it in the trash.

"I'm going to go," Hunter whispered.

"And leave me here with Marie?" I asked.

"It will be bad if I stay any longer."

He was right. I nodded and Hunter left, leaving me in the dark office.

Marie turned the light off again and she walked in my direction. I swallowed the lump in my throat and could barely sit still in my chair even though I tried my hardest to remain cool.

"Looks like you have a long night ahead of you," Marie said, looking at my screen to see how far I was on the project.

I nodded.

"Yeah, I am planning to finish it by tonight," I said.

Marie let out a laugh. "It's funny. I had suspicions that there was something going on between you and Hunter. But I thought it was just in my crazy imagination. It seems like it's not so crazy after all."

"What are you talking about?" I asked, looking in her direction. Her breath reeked of alcohol.

"Don't play, Blue." Marie leaned down to whisper in my ear. "Don't think I'm going to let you get away with this."

My stomach churned at the calmness in her voice and I knew from that instant that she was about to brew up a storm. She reached for the lamp on my desk and turned off my lamp, leaving me in complete darkness. She walked away and left me alone in the dark office. She was trying to intimidate me and it was working. I felt my hands tremble on the keyboard and I had to hold them together to make it stop.

I listened to the sound of the elevator head back to the main floor and there was an eerie silence in the office.

I knew it was a mistake to have let Hunter fuck me in the office. I should've known better, but I let my urges get the best of me and now my life was fucked. I was going to lose everything. Hunter included. But I wasn't worried for myself. I worried for Hunter. I didn't know what Marie was capable of or how far she would go, but I knew she wasn't going to back down. She was going to ruin me, and I hoped that she wasn't going to take Hunter down as well. This firm was Hunter's life, I knew how important it was to him and how much effort it took to build it from the ground up. I had little to lose in comparison to him.

I had promised myself that I was going to finish the project that evening for Marie. But there was no way that I could get anything done after what had just happened. I sat there frozen in fear, staring at my computer screen.

Before I knew it, it was midnight and I wasn't even halfway from finishing. I forgot that I hadn't eaten in twelve hours and my stomach grumbled. But I pushed on and did a little at a time.

It was around six in the morning when I finally finished.

I felt exhausted and I went into the washroom to clean myself up. There were dark circles under my eyes. I used some paper towels to wipe the dewiness off my face and Hunter's sweat that still clung to my arms. I straightened up my outfit. I hoped no one remembered that I was wearing the same thing as I was yesterday. There wasn't any time to go back to my place to change. There was going to be a full day ahead of me before I could go back home. I could feel my exhaustion in all my muscles and my legs still ached from getting fucked the night before. Hunter was so big and he'd fucked me so hard that it was hard for me to walk straight.

When I left the washroom, I noticed that some people had already started coming into the office. I went back to my desk to print off what I'd completed the night before and placed it on Marie's desk. Walking in there and smelling the pungent perfume that she always wore made my legs shake.

Stay strong, Blue. I reminded myself.

There wasn't anything to be afraid of, especially with Hunter upstairs. I knew that he'd protect me from her and everything was going to be okay. But I was delirious from my lack of sleep and even my vision was a bit blurry. When I tried to sit back down, I started getting dizzy.

"You alright, Blue?" Carl, the other project administrator sitting beside me, asked when he walked in.

He'd just arrived in the office and he dropped his bag onto his desk.

"Yeah, just a bit tired," I said.

"Goddamn, you look like shit," he said. "Not to offend you or anything. But what the hell happened?"

"Nothing, I just had to stay late to finish some work. I'll be fine," I said.

But I wasn't, and my arms started to feel so heavy that I couldn't even pick them up without breathing heavily.

I heard whispers behind me. When I turned around, I saw a group of my coworkers in a circle, staring at me with concern. I tried to count how many people there were. But since everything was so blurry, I couldn't even tell who they were.

"He's so pale. Should we call an ambulance?" someone had said.

"I've never seen him like this," someone else added.

It was all a blur, and as I tried to tell them that I was going to be alright. My vision turned black, and the last thing I remembered was my face slamming against the keyboard.

I was lying down somewhere when I woke up, and everything was white. There was a TV playing in the background, and it was the familiar sounds of a soccer game. I blinked a few times to adjust to the blinding fluorescent light.

I was hooked up to a monitor that was measuring my heart rate, and next to it was an IV bag. I licked my chapped lips and tasted a bit of blood on them.

"Yes!" a man yelled out.

I turned to the side to see Harry standing up from his chair. His eyes were glued to the television that was hanging on the wall opposite the bed. Typical Harry. He was so caught up in the game that he didn't even know that I had woken up.

I realized that I was in the hospital. I wondered how long I'd been there for. For all I knew, I could've been in there for weeks.

"Harry," I called out, lifting my head up off the pillow.

I was surprised by how raspy my voice was and how difficult it was to sit up.

"No way, Jose," Harry said, finally turning to me when he noticed that I was awake.

He put his hand on my shoulder to push me back down on the bed.

"There's no food or drink for you, and there's certainly no getting up," Harry said as if he was the doctor himself.

"How long have I been here for?" I asked, clearing my throat.

"One day, and thanks to you, I had to take a day off work. You had me worried sick. You moved out for no more than a few days, and you are already almost dead."

"I am fine," I said.

"Fine? You're paler than a ghost." He scoffed and turned back to the TV before bringing his attention back to me.

"When can I get out?" I asked.

"The doc said when your electrolyte levels get back to normal," Harry said.

I lay there, half paying attention to the game with Harry. When I finally felt more comfortable and awake, all I could think about was Hunter.

"Is Hunter here?" I asked.

Harry shook his head. My heart felt heavy and I wondered if he even knew I was in the hospital.

"He tried to come into the room, but I didn't let him," Harry said.

"Why?" I asked. "Is he still here? Tell him to come in."

Harry crossed his arms and shook his head again.

"There's no way I'm going to let this jerk-off come in to see you," he said.

"Why?" I asked again.

"I knew he was bad news from the moment I met him. Your coworker told me you stayed there all night to finish something. What the hell kind of company works their employee to exhaustion? When Hunter tried to barge into the room, I almost punched him in the face."

I shook my head which was the only part of my body that I could move.

"It wasn't his fault," I said. "I did this to myself."

But Harry wasn't going to listen to anything I had to say. He was more stubborn than a pile of bricks.

I wanted to call out Hunter's name. The only person that I wanted to see was him. I didn't have the energy to fight with Harry. My eyelids felt heavy and I fell back to sleep.

20

HUNTER

I wanted to punch Harry in the face when he denied me entry into Blue's hospital room. He was acting like he was some bouncer in an exclusive club. I told him to go fuck himself. I didn't even care that he was Blue's brother. But I had a hard time trying to figure out just how exactly they were related when they couldn't be more different.

Security escorted me outside for making a scene. I was now sitting outside the hospital and I didn't know what to do.

I should've told Blue to go home that night, I should've stood up for him in front of Marie. But I was scared, fucking terrified that Marie had walked in on us after we just had sex. I was terrified that everyone in the office would find out who I really was. I could lose everything. The company that I'd worked so hard to build. All the clients that I've gained over the years. All because of my inability to control my urges.

Thinking about Blue made my heart pound faster than downing ten cups of coffee. After we fucked last night, it made me want him so much more. But I'd put myself in a bind, I knew that we couldn't continue on like this if he still worked for me. For the first time in my life, I realized that I couldn't have it all. I couldn't have Blue work for me and have a secret relationship with him—if I could even call it a relationship.

I had to choose. I had to give up Blue or my business. It would be an easy decision if it wasn't for how quickly I was falling for Blue.

But could someone really be worth all the time and dedication that I put in Magna? A person could leave me for someone else. A person could change their mind. But my business—my blood, sweat, and tears—that would never go away.

But Blue wasn't just anyone else. He had changed everything I knew about myself in the time that we've known each other. I knew that I could learn so much more with him.

I palmed my face as I sat at a picnic table under the gazebo. The sky was overcast for the first time in a while. The once vibrant leaves of the summer weren't as green today as they were under the sun.

I looked out into the distance to see Harry leaving through the front doors of the hospital. My fists clenched and my immediate reaction was to challenge him to a fight. But I took a deep breath and realized that it wasn't worth it. Causing him pain would only hurt Blue. I had to respect Harry even though I didn't get along with him. He was, after all, Blue's brother.

I watched as Harry got into his tacky red pickup truck and he drove off the lot of the hospital. I was an opportunist, and I realized that it was the perfect time to go see Blue now that Harry was gone. I got up and peered into the windows to see where the security guard was. He was hard to miss because he was almost as tall as me. I spotted him leaning over the receptionist's desk. He was looking like he was flirting with the receptionist who was sitting across from him.

I walked slowly through the automatic doors and kept my eyes on the guard as I snuck past him. Then I made a break for it and ran to the room at the end of the hall where Blue was staying in.

It was a private room and I closed the door gently behind me. The television was on and I wondered if he was awake. I drew the curtains open and I walked toward the bed. He was lying there with his eyes closed. He looked paler than I'd ever seen him before. His golden skin looked washed out and his lips were so pale that they looked white. I leaned in close, putting my hand on his and felt how cold he was.

I wanted to call a nurse to give him another blanket, but I knew I wasn't even supposed to be in there. So, I took off my blazer and put it over him, hoping that he'd warm up. I leaned in close to kiss his lips and ran my hand along his smooth cheek. Even in this state, he looked beautiful. I wanted to throw or punch something. Had Harry come in at that moment, I would've fought him if he gave me any reason to. But I held back my anger and leaned over Blue, stroking his cheek, praying that he'd get better soon.

"I'm sorry," I whispered to him. "I'm sorry for letting this happen to you. I'm sorry that you're in here now because of me."

His chest rose and fell gently in his sleep. He must've been exhausted. I knew he couldn't hear me which was okay because it was the only time I could apologize to him without him knowing. I never said sorry to anyone, I hated apologizing, but I felt like I needed to for Blue. It was me who caused him all this pain and suffering, and I didn't even know how I was ever going to fix it.

I was worried that Harry was going to return. I worried that the guard was going to see me on the cameras. I had to leave soon. I kissed Blue one more time. I left the room and exited through the back door.

I returned back to the office in the afternoon and greeted my receptionist. Usually, she was very friendly, it was the reason why I'd hired her, but today, she barely even looked at me. I wondered if word had gotten out about Blue and me. But I held my head high, hoping that I wasn't overthinking it and I went upstairs to my office.

I left my door open, hoping that my employees would come in and talk to me so I'd get a better sense of what was going on. But the office was oddly silent that day. Blue hadn't been working for me for a long time, but I'd gotten used to having him around in the office. It made the day go by faster knowing that I could go and find him whenever I wanted. I always made excuses to drop by whenever I could. But today felt different because he wasn't there.

I reached inside my desk and pulled out the stress ball I had inside. I clenched it in my fist, feeling it deflate in my palm. I did it a few times before it tore in half and didn't return back to its normal state. I chucked it against the wall watching it bounce off my bookshelf and fall to the ground.

I hated how this situation was outside my control. It was the first time in my life that I'd felt this way. I'd been good at controlling everything around me. I was always in the driver's seat. But I lost that control that day. More than anything, I hated how it felt like I was sky diving and trying to open a parachute that wouldn't open. It felt like I was watching everything around me fall to pieces without being able to do anything about it.

My phone rang and it was Giorgio.

"Hello?" I answered.

"Hey, Hunter! Are you hungry?" Giorgio asked, his voice was so loud from excitement that I had to turn my volume down.

"Not particularly today," I said.

"Well, if you haven't had lunch yet and you're in your office, I am making something. I'm trying out new food ideas for a new lunch menu. You should come over and test it out, I'd love to know what you think."

I stared at the pile of work on my desk that I hadn't touched that day. But I knew it wasn't going to be easy to finish it with Blue on my mind.

"Sure," I said. "I could use the distraction."

I hung up and let the receptionist know before leaving the office. I walked across the street to Giorgio's restaurant. The door was locked and I had to knock on it to get Giorgio's attention.

He let me inside and greeted me with a glass of wine.

"You're going to love what I'm about to serve you," he said, smiling.

I couldn't help but smile at his excitement. Though, I couldn't truly be happy knowing Blue was in the hospital.

"What's wrong?" he asked.

I took a sip of wine.

"Nothing," I said. "Just a lot of work recently."

Giorgio put a hand on my shoulder and squeezed it. "Don't stress, life's too short for that," he said.

"It's easy for you to say with four successful restaurants under your belt."

"Hey, last time I checked, you're doing pretty well yourself, or else I doubt that we'd be friends."

He had a point. But he didn't know that I could lose everything. All because I couldn't control my sexual urges around Blue in the office.

He sat me down at the bar. It was just us in there, not even a single staff member was in the restaurant.

He poured me more wine and put the bottle on the table.

"Trying to get me drunk before noon?" I asked.

"Sure, why not? Looks like you'll need it today, you look rough," he said.

I scratched my beard. It was usually kept to a stubble, but I hadn't had the energy to clean myself up after what happened with Blue.

Giorgio returned to the kitchen and brought down some plates of food.

"I'm hoping to try opening up for lunch at this place. I figured that it's doable, seeing as so many people are out during the day on this street."

"I think there's an opportunity for it, a lot of business people need a place to go to around lunchtime. Most patios I see around here are full during noon."

The food in front of me smelled delicious, and I could've finished it all had I not been thinking so much about Blue.

"What's going on in the office?" Giorgio asked, taking a sip of wine.

I spooned some food onto my empty plate to be polite. I procrastinated from answering his question. I didn't share much with other people. I didn't get the point. But for some reason, I felt like I needed to get it off my chest. And with Giorgio's warm welcome in his beautiful restaurant, I felt comfortable to do so.

"You remember that evening when I had to help the young men who couldn't pay for their meals?" I spoke over the light classical music playing in the background.

Giorgio looked to the ceiling as if he was trying to remember what I was talking about and then smiled and nodded. "Yes, the bastards who didn't have money to pay that night."

"Well, the blond one, his name is Blue. I think I'm starting to fall for him."

Giorgio looked at me with raised brows before sipping more wine.

"Fall for him?" Giorgio repeated. "You mean you're..."

"Gay?" I finished his sentence for him.

Giorgio nodded.

"I thought I'd always been into women until I met him. And now I don't know," I said.

Giorgio reached over and put my hand in his.

"I'm happy you told me this," Giorgio said. "I thought you're sad because of your business but it's just love that you're fretting over."

Giorgio reached to hold my hand. I was hesitant at first but I let him. In our five years of friendship, we'd never touched each other like that. I knew he was trying to let me know that he accepted me for loving another man.

"So, what's the big problem?" Giorgio asked. "You like another man, but why are you so sad?"

I moved the food around my plate, before taking a bite. I realized how delicious the meal that Giorgio prepared was. But I still wasn't hungry. I ate it out of respect for Giorgio.

"It's a problem because I hired him to work for me. I saw potential in him. But other people in the office are starting to suspect what's going on."

"Damn, Hunter. You know better than that. It was you who taught me never to mix business with pleasure."

"I know and I wish I could redo it all over again. I thought that by hiring Blue, I could keep my feelings for him at bay. I thought I'd have enough self-control to not develop any feelings for Blue. I wanted to have a strictly business relationship. But I was wrong. I couldn't help but feel what I felt, especially because I see him every day."

Giorgio sighed, putting more food on my plate when he saw that I'd eaten everything off of it.

"What are you going to do now?" he asked.

"I wish I knew," I said, admitting defeat. "In my current state, I can't make a decision to save my life."

"Well, you need to think about it. With a bit of time, you'll gain a bit of perspective. Figure out what your values are and what's important. There's no doubt that you'll figure it out, I'm sure of it. You're Hunter Cohen, for fuck's sake, you're capable of anything."

I let out a tight smile. Hearing Giorgio's encouragement was great. But even one of my most-respected friends couldn't help me with this problem. I had to figure it out for myself.

Giorgio had continued to bring more food out and we talked a bit about business. I drank more and more wine, and Giorgio being a gracious host kept filling up my glass whenever it was empty. We'd both consumed three bottles by the time I realized how long I had stayed.

"I should really go," I said.

"Okay." Giorgio nodded. "Some of my staff are coming in soon before dinner service, so I should hide these empty bottles so that they don't see it."

I chuckled and got up, feeling a little lightheaded and tipsy.

"Hey, Hunter," Giorgio said. "Come back any time you want to talk about anything. I'm just across the street."

"Sure thing. I didn't know how much I needed you this afternoon."

Giorgio reached out and held me in his arms. It was the first time we'd hugged each other. We only ever shook hands. But it felt good to know that he accepted me after I'd just come out to him.

"Just know that I love you no matter what," Giorgio said. "You're welcome here any time."

I nodded with my face buried in his shoulder.

I ordered an Uber and decided to head home, I was too drunk to work anyway and too upset over Blue to get anything done. I'd put too much on my plate. Being too busy was the reason why I remained single for so long. It was difficult to juggle an enterprise on top of a relationship, especially one that was brand new to me. It was my first relationship with another man and I didn't know how to act or feel in it.

I waited outside on the patio for the Uber to arrive and headed home.

The overcast sky washed out all the colors in my apartment when I walked in. But I was too tipsy for any kind of daylight anyway. With a touch of a button, I was able to close all of my blinds so that I could be in complete darkness. I went into my bathroom and stripped, feeling the cool marble tiles on my feet. I ran my hand on my beard and looked into the mirror. It was different from how clean I usually looked. I filled the tub up with warm water, knowing that a bath was going to help me get rid of my headache.

When the tub was filled, I dipped my feet in. The water was hotter than expected, but I got inside anyway. It was nice to be distracted by something other than the heartache of seeing Blue in the hospital. I wasn't a religious man, but I closed my eyes to pray for his recovery. The water felt like it was burning my skin. But I eventually got used to it and I rested my head onto the side of the tub, listening to the rhythmic drip of the faucet. When I closed my eyes, I pictured Blue's face when I fucked him in the office. Instantly, my cock hardened in the warm water. I ran my hand on my shaft, stroking myself to the thought of Blue's lusty eyes. I pictured the way he bit his lips when I fucked him hard. I wished that he was there in that moment, but I wished that more than anything he got better so that we could do it again. My hand was not nearly as pleasurable as being inside Blue's ass. Nothing could beat his tight hole that clenched onto my cock. I groaned at the thought of fucking him again. There was so much more that I wanted to do with him, there was so much more that we needed to explore.

I stroked myself harder, making violent waves in the water with my hand on my shaft. My toes curled as my drunken imagination of Blue's body grew wilder.

"Blue," I groaned with my eyes closed in my empty bathroom.

My body tightened and I erupted come all over my chest and abs.

I took a deep breath and opened my eyes, using my hands to wash the come off my body.

21

BLUE

I woke up in the hospital again. It was nighttime and the room was lit up by the bright television screen that was left muted.

I could smell the familiar woody scent and a hint of cologne. The scent was immediately recognizable.

"Hunter?" I called out.

There was silence except for the beeping heart monitor beside me.

I looked down to see there was something covering my body. It was then when I realized where Hunter's strong scent was coming from. His blazer was covering me. I knew it was his by putting my nose to it. I closed my eyes and imagined that he was there.

I faintly remembered dreaming about him. Maybe when I was dreaming, he was actually in the hospital with me. How else would he have left his blazer here? In the dream, he had said something to me but I couldn't remember for the life of me what he'd said.

The emptiness of the eerie hospital room made my body feel cold, and I used Hunter's blazer for comfort.

"Hunter? Are you there?" I called out again.

But this time, a nurse had walked into the room.

"Is everything okay?" she asked, signing her initials on the clipboard that was hanging on the wall.

"I guess so," I said.

She came over and checked the monitor, and then put a hand over my forehead like my mom used to do when I was sick.

"Can I get out of here yet?" I asked, trying to move my legs that had fallen asleep under the blanket.

"The doctor said tomorrow, but you better get some rest tonight. When you wake up, your brother will come and get you."

I nodded and asked her to hand me the remote that was on the armrest of the chair where Harry had been sitting. I wondered where he was.

The night passed by slowly as I tried to sleep, but all I could think about was Hunter. I flipped through the channels. It was hard trying to find something to watch and I ended up settling on some cartoons. I wrapped Hunter's blazer closer toward me and pretended like I was in his arms.

I missed Hunter's touch. But I knew that things were never going to be the same again. I was worried about Hunter more than I was for myself. I was sure that Marie would have said something to other people at the office.

The words that she whispered in my ear that night she caught us still gave me chills. *Don't think I'm going to let you get away with this.*

I'd gotten a bit more sleep before I was woken up by Harry tapping my shoulder.

"Time to go, loser," he said.

I smiled, even though he called me a loser. I was glad that I could get out of there. There were some release forms that I had to sign. Harry had brought me some clothes so that I could change into them. I sat up on the bed and I put my feet on the ground for the first time in what felt like forever. It felt like sharp needles pricking into my feet as I regained blood circulation in my legs.

I walked into the bathroom and changed. I was surprised at how much better I looked since staying up all night in the office. The circles under my eyes were not as dark, and my skin wasn't as pale as it was a couple days ago. I put on my clothes and stepped outside where Harry was talking to the doctor in the hallway.

"Are you going to be okay by yourself?" he asked.

"I'll be fine," I said. "Don't worry about me."

"You said that when you moved out of my apartment and look what happened."

I didn't have the energy to argue with him and all I could think about was when I could see Hunter again.

"What day of the week is it?" I asked.

"Wednesday," Harry said, palming the steering wheel. "Why?"

"Just thinking about when I'd be able to get back to work again."

"You're seriously thinking of going back to work for that motherfucker?" Harry asked.

"It wasn't his fault that I passed out. If anything, it was my manager who'd given me the work on such a tight deadline."

"Either way, I think you should seriously reconsider going back there. Is it really worth it to risk your health for a paycheck? There are other jobs out there. Hell, if you want to work in construction, we're hiring all the time."

I glanced over at Harry. "I can't work in construction. Are you nuts?"

"Why not? Maybe you'll be less of a wuss. It'll help you build some character."

I hated Harry and I loved him at the same time.

"Gray's in town, by the way, he came into the city because he was worried about you," Harry mentioned.

"What? Isn't he in Hong Kong?" I asked.

I was surprised to hear that my oldest brother, Gray, had flown halfway around the world to see me.

"Yes, he's your brother and he's concerned about you. I would've done the same thing."

I hadn't seen Gray in years since he moved to Asia for business. He was fifteen years older than me, and because of our age gap, I wasn't as close to him as I was to Harry.

"Where is he staying?" I asked.

"At a Marriott by my place," Harry said.

"Maybe we should go to meet him there," I said.

"If that's what you want. I just figured you needed some rest at your own apartment."

"I'll be fine," I said. "Does Mom and Dad know that he's here?"

Harry nodded. "One big happy family, all back together in one city."

I knew he was being sarcastic because our family was sometimes dysfunctional as hell. But there was a bit of truth to what he was saying. Everyone loved each other the best way they knew how.

22

HUNTER

Yet again, it was impossible for me to get anything done at work that day. Blue was on my mind, and there was nothing I could do to focus on any of the projects that were on my desk.

After a while of pacing by the window, I decided to go to the hospital to see if he was okay. When I arrived, I searched to see if Harry's truck was there. Sure enough, I saw his red pickup parked near the front entrance. I hated how he was like some kind of gatekeeper that blocked me from seeing Blue.

It'd been a couple days since Blue was in there. I was sure that he was able to leave now. I remained in the car, trying to figure out what in the hell I should do. If I went inside and saw Harry, I knew that we'd get in a fight. My body was already tense thinking about it. I knew that he would be tense too with Blue in the hospital.

The rational part of me was telling me to just head back to the office and wait for Blue to contact me. But I wasn't someone who waited around for anything. I needed to see him. I needed to make sure that he was okay.

The impatient part of me wanted to burst in there, and run right into Blue's room. I'd be surprised if I'd be able to get away with it. I was sure that security and Harry were going to kick my ass.

I parked my car in a spot where I could watch people walk in and out of the hospital. Someone with bright red hair caught my eye. It was Harry. Then, walking out the front door next to him was Blue. He had my blazer wrapped around him. I couldn't help but smile to see Blue walk out of there. He looked much better than he did when I saw him yesterday. He wasn't as pale and his pink lips looked so kissable.

I got out of my car and I raced toward his direction.

"Blue," I called out.

He turned to me and his smile was brighter than the mid-August sun.

I ran up toward him, but I was stopped with a firm hand on my shoulder.

"Get away from my brother," Harry shouted.

He pushed me so hard that I nearly fell backwards. Harry stood between Blue and me. There was anger in Harry's eyes.

My fists clenched and it was nearly impossible to hold back all the tension I've felt these past few days.

Blue got between us before I did something I regretted. Blue put his hand on my fist and uncurled my fingers to hold my hand in his.

"Don't," he whispered in my ear.

He soothed me with his soft touch that radiated all throughout my body. I was so happy to see him.

"Why are you here?" Harry asked me.

"I came to see Blue," I said.

"And what? What else do you want from him?" Harry asked.

I looked into Blue's crystal eyes and seeing him well again was everything I needed.

"I need nothing from him," I said.

Harry must have noticed how happy Blue and I looked to be reunited. "I don't know anything about you, Hunter. But let me tell you, if anything bad happens to my brother again, I won't let you get away with it."

I brought Blue closer into my arms. For the first time, I didn't care that we were showing affection in public. All I wanted to do was hold his delicate body in my arms.

"I won't let anything happen to your brother," I said.

I reached my hand out and Harry looked at it like it was a foreign object. But after hesitating for a second, he shook my hand.

"I'll be alright," Blue said to Harry.

Harry nodded. "Do you still need me to take you home?"

Blue shook his head. "I want to spend a bit of time with Hunter. But thank you for everything you've done these past couple of days."

"No need to thank me. You're my bro," Harry said.

I knew Harry was a good guy. I'd always known that. Blue was lucky to have such a protective brother in his life. Harry didn't have to worry, I was also going to protect Blue with all my heart.

Harry went back to his truck and I brought Blue to my car.

"Are you hungry?" I asked Blue, helping him get into the passenger seat.

"Not really," he said. "The doctor said I can't eat anything except soup anyway."

"Can I take you back to my place? I will make you some soup then," I said.

Blue smiled. "Since when did you make soup?"

I smirked. "Since today."

After I got him settled in my car, I drove us back to my condo. Blue looked tired and he rested his head against the window.

"I missed you so much," I said. "I didn't know how much I did until you weren't around."

Blue reached out to hold my hand that wasn't on the steering wheel. "I know you tried to see me the other day and I know Harry gave you shit for it."

"I'm just glad that you're okay. I want you to take as much time as you need to rest before going back into the office," I said.

"I was hoping to return tomorrow, I know I overworked myself, but I'll be fine," Blue said.

I shook my head. "It's better if you rest for at least a day or two. Work comes second. Your well-being comes first."

It had never been that way for me. Work was always first in my mind, but I wasn't going to let Blue suffer again. It wasn't worth it to see someone I cared about like this.

We arrive back to my condo and Blue's eyes widened as we went underground to the parking lot.

"You live here?" he asked.

I smiled. "Hell yeah, I do."

We rode the elevator upstairs to my floor and Blue flung his arms around me as soon as we got into the unit.

Blue kissed me before I had the chance to close the front door.

"Hold on there, monkey," I said. "What did the doctor say about strenuous activity?"

"Well, he said I should rest. But who said kissing had to be strenuous?"

Feeling the heat of Blue's body, and his lusty eyes was too much for me to handle. I picked up his legs and wrapped them around me to carry him into the bedroom.

23

BLUE

Hunter was trying to be as gentle with me as he could. But lying in a hospital bed for two days with nothing to do was like I'd just gotten out of jail. I missed Hunter so much. All I had in the hospital was the scent of Hunter's blazer. Now that he was in front of me, I couldn't control myself. I took off his clothes as fast as I could. Hunter took mine off slowly.

I could see Hunter's throbbing cock, and mine was aching as well.

"You sure you want to do this?" Hunter asked.

"I *need* you, Hunter. You don't understand. *Please,* fuck me again," I said, sounding more desperate than I would've liked to.

Being in Hunter's bedroom made me feel safe. It looked like a bank vault with heavy steel doors. There were no windows and sound didn't travel very far in there. But our loud groans still filled the room.

Hunter spread my cheeks open and I felt his finger at my opening.

"I hope I didn't hurt you last time," he said.

I shook my head, and though Hunter fucking me was a bit painful, the insatiable pleasure I felt during it was worth it. He spat onto my hole and rubbed it with his finger. I felt pressure as he inserted it inside me and I felt my body tense up from how much it hurt.

"Relax, baby," he said, already taking the lead after having sex just one time with another man.

Hunter had a powerful energy that commanded respect in the office. His voice was so deep and soothing. I took a few deep breaths as he fingered me deeper. He probed his finger until he touched my prostate. Pre-come started to leak all over my body. I moaned in ecstasy and that only made him finger me harder.

"Your ass is incredible," he said.

He turned me over. I looked down to see his pulsing cock and the mess that he made from his pre-come all over his sheets. I turned back to look at Hunter. His eyes were filled with passion as he concentrated on my body. It reminded me of the times in the office when I'd sneak upstairs to watch him work.

"Ready for two fingers?" Hunter asked.

I bit my lower lip in anticipation for it, and I felt more pressure as he stretched me open with two fingers. But the pain of his thick fingers was too much and I cried out. Hunter retreated quickly.

"You're so tight," Hunter said, kissing the small of my back. "Relax."

I tried to breathe, but because there were so many things on my mind, I couldn't fully let my body loose. He tried again, this time spitting on his fingers, and I felt both his fingers slide into me. I tilted my head back as he entered inside of me.

Hunter leaned forward and kissed me, then reached for the condom and lube in the bedside table.

I turned around and I touched his thighs that felt as sturdy and wide as tree trunks. Hunter slowly rolled the condom on his shaft.

"I couldn't wait to do this in privacy. In this room, you can yell as loud as you want," he said.

My heart beat faster as he lowered his cock to direct it inside my hole.

Hunter put each of my legs on his shoulders. His body looked massive as he leaned over me. I grabbed the sheets as Hunter pushed his cock inside.

I clawed the sheets harder. Hunter leaned in close, kissing me, and drove his hips into me. I felt his cock slowly fill me up inside and his tip brushed against my prostate. Pre-come leaked uncontrollably out of my cock onto my abs.

Hunter wiped some of it off with his hand, and brought it to my mouth, making me taste my own pre-come.

"So sexy," he groaned, followed by deep thrusts inside me.

"It feels so good, Hunter," I cried out.

"You don't even know how great your ass feels," Hunter groaned and grunted. *"I love you so much."*

My eyes widened and I wasn't sure if I heard him correctly.

"What did you just say?" I asked, wiping the sweat off my forehead. I wasn't sure if it was my sweat or Hunter's.

"I said, I love you, Blue. I love you so much."

At that moment, Hunter's cock was so deep inside of me that I felt whole for the first time in a while.

"Really?" I asked.

He nodded and just so I wasn't mistaken he said those words

again. "I love you, Blue. I never thought I'd say this to another man, but I do."

I grabbed the back of his neck to kiss him. Hunter fucked me harder and faster and I knew what was coming next.

"I want you to swallow my load this time," Hunter said. "I want you to taste me."

I couldn't say no to him.

He pumped a dozen more times before he pulled out of me and ripped the condom off his shaft and threw it next to his bed. He kneeled over me so that his cock was right on my lips, and I felt his body tense up before he released his load in my mouth. I closed my eyes and I swallowed his warm come. The bitter warm fluid coated my throat. It was the first time that I'd eaten anything in days. Hunter's come satisfied my hunger and I stroked myself to my own climax.

Hunter collapsed next to me as we breathed heavily next to each other.

"That was incredible," Hunter said.

"I'm glad you think so," I said.

He looked over at me and raised his eyebrows.

"You enjoyed it too, right?" he asked.

"I did, Hunter. But there's something I want to talk to you about, and it's still on my mind."

"What is it, baby, you can tell me now." Hunter palmed my chest with one of his hands which made my heart warm.

"I want to know what's going to happen with us at work. Does Marie know what we did in the office?" I asked.

"I was trying to avoid this conversation. Thinking about it makes me sick," Hunter said, squeezing the bridge of his nose.

"But we have to get through it," I said. "We can't just brush it under the rug."

"I know. But for the first time in my life, I don't know what to do," he said. "I fucked up, I shouldn't have fucked you in the office knowing there was a risk of someone seeing us."

"It's my fault too, I couldn't control my urges for you," I said.

"Neither of us could," he said.

"Thinking about going to work and having to face the entire office and Marie scares me. I don't think I can do it."

"Don't think like that," Hunter said, moving his hand from my chest to my face. "We're in this together now."

"But Marie..." I said, before I paused to think of what I was going to say, I didn't want to sound weak but it was my truth. "Marie is awful to work with, I don't think I can do it anymore. She hates me and I don't know why. I know she's not going to make this any easier for me any time soon."

"I know Marie's like that and she's always been that way."

I turned my body to face Hunter. "So what are you saying, are you saying that I'm going to have to continue working with her?"

Hunter took a deep breath, then nodded. "What do you want me to do? Fire her? She's done nothing wrong and she's been with me for over ten years."

I knew Hunter was in a difficult situation.

"There's no way I'm letting my longest employee go. Marie's a tough woman, but she cares about my business as much as I do," he said.

I shook my head in disbelief. Only I knew the subtle things she did that hurt me.

"I suspected that this conversation would go nowhere. I wish we talked about this before we had sex," I said.

"Why's that?" Hunter asked.

Our bodies moved further away from each other on the king-sized bed.

"I don't think you'll ever choose me over your own business. I can't be with someone who's not going to protect me from an abusive supervisor."

Hunter furrowed his brows and he looked sadder than I'd ever seen him. "You didn't even say it back when I said I love you."

"Because I knew that this was going to happen. Hunter, I've put other people first before me my entire life. It's time for me to stick up for myself and stand up for what I believe in. I can't work at your company and have a secret relationship with you. I don't think you even know what it means to tell someone you love them."

Hunter sat up and rested his head against the headboard. His eyes were glazed over as if he was contemplating what I'd just said.

"Maybe you're right, Blue. You deserve someone who can love you better than I can. I've never said I love you to someone. I only said it because I thought it was the right thing to say. I don't think I know what love is."

Tears streamed out of my eyes uncontrollably when I heard him say that. I knew the conversation I was planning to have that evening wasn't going to be easy. But I wasn't expecting this to happen.

"I should go and I think I should quit my job as well. It was a bad idea to take it in the first place."

Hunter shook his head. "I put you in this mess, Blue. It's not your fault."

His voice was shaky and I'd never seen his shoulders so rounded forward before. Hunter got off the bed. He opened the door to the hallway and disappeared into the bathroom.

I sat on his bed, wiping the tears from my face. I decided that I had to go. It was time. There was nothing else to say to each other.

I put my clothes back on and walked out of his room. I put my ear on the bathroom door and heard Hunter in the shower.

I let myself out of his unit and took the elevator back down to the lobby. A couple entered from the fifth floor and they looked like they were dressed to go out for the evening. The woman was wearing a drapey red dress and nude heels. The man was wearing a dark blue dress shirt that was tucked into a dark pair of jeans. They were so caught up in each other's company that they didn't even notice that I was in the elevator. Their touching and whispers into each other's ear made me want to throw up. I hated how happy they looked, and I hated how miserable I felt. All I wanted to do was go back to my apartment and curl up in my bed.

I couldn't believe that I put myself in the same situation as the one that'd hurt me in the first place. I put my heart in another man's hands when my heart was already fragile, cracked, and bruised. I was back to square one, unemployed, and alone. I had no idea how I was going to pay rent without a job. I'd probably have to move back into my brother's apartment. The more I thought about it, the more I could see why Harry had been so protective of me.

Hunter disappointed me because I thought he was different. I thought that I could be happy with him. I was wrong. But I was glad that I had the courage to talk to him about it instead of just ignoring how I felt which was what I usually did. Standing up for myself was the one thing that had me holding my head a little higher on my way home.

24

HUNTER

I couldn't bear looking at Blue cry. I didn't want to be next to him at that moment because I was hurt too and I didn't want Blue to see me broken. I never let anyone see me in pain. I never showed weakness and so I did what I knew how to do best, which was to run from my problems.

I had always used my work as a way to cover up my inability to have genuine relationships. I left the bedroom knowing that it wouldn't solve anything. But it gave me a chance to get out of there so that Blue didn't get a chance to see me weak.

I looked at myself in the mirror in the bathroom and all I could see was how much of a failure I was. I didn't even know why I had put myself in this position in the first place. I didn't think I would ever see Blue again after that night at his brother's apartment...let alone fall in love with him. That was the reason why I hired him. I thought I owed it to him as an apology. But my feelings for him had spiraled out of control.

I felt bad for Blue. If he only knew how much I was hiding beneath the walls I put up, he'd know how broken I really am. Maybe he wouldn't even be spending so much time with me. He deserved someone better, *someone who was capable of loving him.*

I let the water wash the sweat off my skin in the shower and I closed my eyes feeling the warm water blanket my body. I tried to clear my mind of thoughts, but all I could think about was Blue. I never second-guessed myself, but for once in my life, I wonder if I'd made a mistake.

I arrived in the office later than usual. It was hard getting out of bed, especially since my sheets smelled of Blue. But I knew that I couldn't run from my problems any longer. I went to the third floor to see that Blue wasn't there. I knew he was never coming back.

Marie was in her office and I could see the smile on her face. There was a bitter taste in my mouth, seeing her look so content and knowing how much she'd been hurting Blue.

I walked into her office that smelled of her perfume.

"Marie, I'd like to see you in my office immediately," I said.

She looked up at me, confused.

"What's it about?" she asked. "Why can't we discuss it here?"

"Don't ask any more questions until you come to my office," I said.

I could be firm with a lot of people. But Marie, because she reminded me of my mother, was the one person I let slip away with everything.

She followed me up to my office and I closed the door behind us. I sat down at my desk and Marie sat across from me. She crossed her legs and put her hands on her lap, but she never wiped the grin off her face.

"I want you to know that what you've been doing to Blue has been unfair," I said. "I don't tolerate that kind of culture here and you know it."

Her smile got wider. "What I've been doing with Blue? Let's talk about what *you've* been doing with Blue."

She had tricks up her sleeve and I wasn't prepared for her to put the spotlight back on me.

"What are you talking about," I said, crossing my arms.

"Oh, you know I'm not stupid, Hunter. I knew you *fucked* him that night."

My face turned hot and I wasn't expecting her to just flat out say it like that.

"Can we talk about that? Having sex in the office, is that the culture that you're tolerating?" she asked.

"No," I said, firmly. "I'm hoping you have the decency to keep that to yourself. But that's not what we're here to talk about. I wanted to talk about how Blue was sent to the hospital because you overworked him."

"We are talking about Blue," Marie said. "But really, if Blue was competent, he wouldn't have needed to stay all night to finish that project. Anyone could've finished that easily."

She knew that wasn't true, but I also knew how cutthroat she was. It was how she'd made it to the top in this industry. I had her in such a powerful position for a reason, but now it was backfiring against me.

"Look, whatever you might think, I want you to know that it's not going to work out with you here anymore," I said. "So I urge that you consider resigning before things get out of hand."

I was surprised to see her so calm after what I'd said and she continued to smile.

"Resign? Who do you think I am, Hunter? Just because you're the CEO doesn't mean you know more than me. I have twenty years of experience more than you, and you think I'm just going to coward out without a fight? You really want to go this route, when I have all the evidence in the world to ruin you?"

I backed into my chair. Even though I was so much bigger than her, Marie had a way of saying things. I'd seen her in important meetings. Her stillness, like the calm before a storm, was what fucked with my head.

"Don't think this is over just like that, Hunter. I'm not like Blue, I don't cower in a corner. After all the years we've worked together, you, of all people, should know that." She smirked. "I didn't even know you were *gay*."

She knew exactly how to get under my skin.

"I'm not gay," I said, in a low voice.

She had me figured out, when this whole time, I thought I was coy about it.

"Then I must be crazy, I see the way you look at Blue, the way you touch him when you think no one is watching. I see everything. But the sad thing is that I thought we had a future together."

"What are you talking about?" I asked with my brows furrowed.

"We had a chance together. We could've taken your business

far together. But you chose a little boy over a woman," Marie said, running her hand through her grey hair. "I loved you, Hunter. I still do and I won't let you get your little happily ever after with that twerp. I told you it was a bad idea to hire him. I warned you. Didn't I?"

"What are you going to do, Marie? I don't see you like that. We've always had a professional relationship and it was simply that. What in your right mind made you think that we'd be together?"

"Oh, it was always my plan. You think I'd still be working here if I didn't want you? When you hired Blue, I knew he'd cause you distractions. I saw how you were looking at him in the interview, and I wasn't going to let it happen. But it did. Now you're pinning everything on me. Everything is *your fault.* Just own it."

I shook my head in disbelief. "It was your fault that Blue ended up in the hospital. He was just trying to meet your impossible standards."

She let out a laugh. "I want to ask you one more thing. Can there ever be something between us?"

I looked her dead in the eyes and shook my head. "No."

"Well, then. I have my answer," Marie said.

She stood up and walked to the door. Marie looked over her

shoulder one more time at me before she left my office and closed the door.

I palmed my face. I thought it would go differently, and I didn't know what she was going to do next, but I knew what she was capable of. She was going to ruin me and everything I'd worked so hard for. But I couldn't just fire her that easily. She could sue me for wrongful termination and I was aware of that. She covered her tracks well.

I was surprised when she'd confessed her love to me. I suddenly knew why she'd been so cruel to Blue, it was because she hated how much potential I saw in him. She hated how much love I had for him. I felt as if she'd backed me into a corner.

I looked at all the awards that I displayed proudly in my office. I looked at the archived projects that I poured my heart and soul into. I once felt the most powerful in my office. But now, it felt like Marie had set everything on fire in front of me.

Was it worth the battle?

Was my twenty years of work worth seeing Blue smile again? seeing the optimistic way he saw the world? seeing him laugh?

Without a doubt.

I would leave it all behind me for the chance to tell him that I loved him again. That was the truth. It was *my truth*. Marie wasn't going to intimidate me. I was ready to face her head on.

When I went back down to the third floor, I noticed that it was oddly quiet. When I turned the corner, I realized it was because nobody was there, including Marie. I panicked as I went down to the lobby and saw that the entire office had assembled in the boardroom. I could hear Marie's voice, and she was just finishing up her speech. She was sitting at the head of the table.

I didn't know what she'd said. I walked into the boardroom and noticed my employees avoiding eye contact. I knew it was bad. The only person that was looking at me was Marie. She walked up to me and put her hand on my shoulder.

"Now, I quit," she said. "Is anyone coming with me?"

I was expecting every single person to have left the boardroom with her. But I was surprised to see that everyone remained standing or seated.

Marie's eyes widened and looked at me one more time before walking away toward the front doors. Her heels clicked against the marble floors.

I took a deep breath and my employees looked at me, some with confused faces, and some looked sorry for me.

"We accept you, Mr. Cohen," someone said.

"We saw how Marie was treating Blue, and he was the nicest guy in the world. It was wrong of her," another employee added.

"We don't care if you're interested in Blue," another voice in the crowd said. "I think you should go for him!"

My employees exited the boardroom, and I looked down onto the ground, unable to look them in the eyes. But one by one, people let me know that they were on my side and that they trusted me. I was reminded of why I'd hired each person on my team. They were people I believed in, and just as importantly, people who believed in me. And even though Blue wasn't there that day, I could say the same thing about him as well.

People went back to their desks and resumed their day as normal. I knew there would be conversations in the office about what had happened. But at the end of the day, I knew that I had a team of people who supported me. They supported me for loving Blue.

I left the office early that day. I headed right for Blue's apartment, I hoped that he was there because he was the only person that I wanted to see. The front door was locked and I tried to use the intercom directory to find Blue's name but it wasn't on the list yet. I had stopped by a convenience store on the way there when I saw a beautiful display of red roses outside. I bought a dozen of them for him and I was holding them in my hands.

"Are you trying to get inside?" a lady asked, pushing a cart full of groceries.

"Yes," I said, smiling at the woman with white hair and glasses.

"Well, based on how you're dressed, it doesn't look like you're trying to break and enter," she said, looking at my roses.

"Nope, just trying to mend a broken heart, that's all."

She put in the code and the door opened, I let her in first.

"Well, I hope she's happy to see you. A woman always loves roses," she said.

I was going to nod and smile, but I decided to say something instead.

"It's for a man, actually," I said, correcting her.

"Oh, well I'm sure he's a lucky man to be receiving them."

"I sure hope so. But really, I'm the lucky man."

We entered the elevator together and she got off on the second floor, wishing me good luck. I rode the rest of the way to the top. I walked down the hallway to Blue's apartment, and I paused before knocking on his door. I asked myself if I was sure of this decision. It was going to forever change the course of my life and the answer was yes. I gently tapped on the door and I waited for Blue to open it.

I heard footsteps approach and Blue's face peering in from the crack. His eyes lit up when he saw me.

"Hunter? What are you doing here?" he asked.

I smiled and handed him the roses that I kept hidden behind my back. "I came to see you. Can I come in?"

He hesitated, looking at the flowers before he nodded and let me enter his apartment. It was still unfurnished for the most part and half-empty boxes scattered on the ground. I noticed that the bed that Blue ordered had arrived.

"These are beautiful," Blue said, holding the roses up in the kitchen.

He took the vase that was sitting on top of the fridge and filled it with water and he put the flowers in them.

"I'm glad you think so." I smiled, sitting on the foot of his bed since he didn't have any chairs.

"Did you come just to give me these?" he asked.

"No. I came to tell you that after what happened last night. I really thought about what you said and what you want...and I want to try and give it to you. I want to compromise because I see a future with you, Blue. Really, what I'm trying to say is, I can't see a future *without* you."

He smiled, his eyes cast down onto the ground before looking back up at me.

"I want a future with you too," he said.

"Marie left today after a conversation we had. I couldn't stand the pain she caused you. I realized that I can't have someone work for me who doesn't respect the man I love."

"You really did that?" Blue asked.

I nodded. "She didn't leave without making a scene, and....I'm afraid people at the office know more than they should. But in the end, it worked out, because everyone supported us. My biggest fear was people finding out that I was...gay. But I realized today that I care more about being with the man I love than what other people think of me. I love you, Blue."

"Hunter, I love you too," Blue said for the first time.

He walked toward me and sat next to me on the bed.

"I'm *sorry* that I ever put business ahead of the special bond we had together," I said.

It'd never been easy for me to apologize, but I needed Blue to know how I truly felt for him.

"I forgive you, Hunter. I knew that for this to work, I had to finally stand up for myself and for what I believe is right. Had I stayed silent, I wouldn't have been happy and that would've affected us."

I kissed his lips and nodded to let him know that I understood him. I put his hand in mine. I knew how delicate he was. He was more delicate than the roses that I'd gotten for him. I loved that about him. I brought Blue's hands to my heart to let him feel how fast my heart was beating.

"This is how scared I am about loving you, Blue. Loving another man for the first time. I'm going to need your guidance through this because the concept of love is new to me. I've never opened myself up to someone and I'm ready to for you."

Blue pulled my hand toward his chest, and I felt his beating heart as well.

"And I'm just as scared as you, but we can do it together," he said.

I smiled and kissed him again. "I don't want to rush into anything, but I want you to know that you should return to the office when you're ready."

"I can't," Blue said, shaking his head. "Everyone knows what happened, and I can't face it, it'll be too embarrassing."

"I know," I said, reassuring him. "But this afternoon, when Marie made her exit, she tried to get everyone to come with her. But they chose us over her, people there love you, and they should, because they see how great of a person you are."

"They really think I'm a good person?" Blue asked.

I nodded. "I'm going to spend the rest of my life telling you how amazing you are."

Seeing Blue smile again was more important than any project that I'd ever worked on.

25

BLUE

I was happy to be with Hunter again, and we spent most of that evening lying in bed with Hunter holding me in his arms.

"I love you," I said softly.

"I love you, too, Blue," Hunter said back to me. "I'm happy to hear you say those words. They mean more to me than I thought they would."

Hunter held me closer, kissing me on my forehead and I felt safe.

"I thought I'd never love again after my previous relationship," I said. "I didn't think it was worth it to be vulnerable with another man."

"Was he that bad to you?" Hunter asked, running his hand gently up and down my back.

"He had his own demons, his own addictions, and they were bigger than him. But he took it out on me—on our relationship—and it ruined us. It got worse when he turned to harder drugs."

"I know that feeling when an addiction overtakes your whole body, your soul. Gambling was my addiction and I replaced that with work."

"Will you ever go back to gambling?" I asked.

"Never, I've hit rock bottom because of it and I'll never go back down the same path. But overworking...that's something I'm still trying to balance."

Hunter took a deep breath as I put my head on his chest.

"What do you think you're running away from by working so much?" I asked.

"I don't know. I just know that when I'm alone in my condo, without things to do, that's when my darkest thoughts consume me. That's when I feel like I'm losing it."

"You're enough, Hunter. More than enough, you have nothing to prove to this world."

"No one has ever told me that before. My parents have never

said that they were proud of me. Even with gambling, all I wanted to do was prove to them that I could make it on my own. But now that I have a successful business, I realized that this void I was trying to fill wasn't about money at all. It's because I thought I wasn't good enough. But being with you, Blue, you make me feel whole."

I smiled and kissed him.

"And you're the one who showed me that I'm capable of loving again," I said. "You gave me a chance and the confidence that allowed me to pick myself up and start again. Had I not met you, I may have just given up. I would still be sleeping on Harry's couch. You saved me, Hunter."

We locked lips again. I lay against Hunter's strong body, as he wrapped his arms around me tightly. A tear rolled down my cheek and fell onto Hunter's face.

"Why are you crying?" Hunter asked, wiping my cheek with his finger. "Are you upset about something?"

"No," I said, smiling. "I'm just overwhelmed at how lucky I feel to be with someone who's so perfect."

"You know my flaws, Blue. I'm not perfect," Hunter said in his low voice.

"You're perfect for me, and there's nothing more that I need."

"You better stop talking and kiss me right now, you're making me feel all sappy inside and I hate feeling things."

I listened and I leaned down to brush my lips against his gently to tease him before he pulled me down toward him. I opened my mouth to let his tongue in. I could never get over how great he tasted and how much he always left me wanting more. Hunter was my drug.

Our kiss was interrupted by a knock on the door.

"Who's it?" Hunter yelled, annoyed that someone was interrupting our moment.

"Your pizza is here," the man on the other side of the door yelled back.

Hunter sighed and grunted. I'd totally forgotten that we ordered it half an hour ago.

"I'll get it," Hunter said.

"Not with that showing." I smiled, pointing to his raging-hard cock that was visible from a mile away.

He reached in his pants and tucked in his hard-on in the waistband of his underwear. I laughed as he walked awkwardly toward the door.

"Thank you," I heard Hunter say and accepting the box of pizza.

He closed the door and brought it back to the bed.

"You know, I should consider moving in with you," Hunter said.

I opened the box of pepperoni pizza and my stomach grumbled at the sight of the delicious cheese wheel. Though kissing Hunter was satisfying, I still had to remember to eat.

"You want to move in with me?" I asked. "Don't you mean you want me to move into your place?"

"No," Hunter said. "I love how simple your life is, I am happy just eating pizza off a mattress on the floor. I don't need a bank vault for a bedroom, I don't need a multimillion-dollar penthouse suite. All I need is you."

I smiled, grabbing a slice of pizza that was too hot for my fingers but I put it in my mouth anyway.

"We'll talk about it, but I'm sure we at least need a couch and a table in here. We're not going to be just sleeping on my bed all the time."

"Why not? I could be on this bed forever with you," Hunter said with his familiar smirk.

"Maybe you're right," I said.

We ate a few slices and Hunter went to the kitchen to wash his hands. On his way back, he noticed one of my boxes that was open. He paused before squatting down to take a closer look.

"What are you looking at?" I asked.

"This work...Blue, is this yours?"

I knew he was referring to the box of artwork that I'd worked on in college and up until my breakup with my ex. I nodded.

"I knew you were talented. But I had no idea you were this creative," Hunter said, pulling out a painting from the box to take a closer look.

I went over to him to see what he was looking at, it was a mock marketing campaign that I did for a Japanese clothing brand. They were watercolor paintings and sketches of my vision.

"Why in the world haven't I seen this before?" Hunter asked.

"I don't show people. It's never really gotten me anywhere. When I applied for jobs after finishing school, no one really cared about my portfolio. I didn't know how to apply what I learned, so I just picked up practical jobs to pay the bills."

"Blue, you applied for Project Administrator at my company. But really, you should be in the creative department. We need someone like you with fresh eyes to make our proposals stand out."

"You really think I can be in the creative department?" I asked with my brows raised.

"Blue, it's where you belong. I know it was a struggle for you to work under Marie...but were you even interested in the work?"

I didn't want to admit the truth, but I trusted Hunter to tell him how I really felt.

"I hated it, but I did it because I didn't want to let you down."

Hunter furrowed his brows. "I want you to switch departments. When you're ready to return back to work, I am going to have you work under John, the creative director. John's a great guy and he's different from Marie, more caring and empathetic, and he'll help you get started."

I took a deep breath, I hated change, and I'd always played my cards as safely as possible. But being safe hadn't gotten me anywhere and Hunter was pushing me to do great things. Things that I was actually passionate about, instead of getting by day after day.

"Okay," I said. "If you trust me, I'll do it."

"You know I trust you, Blue. But you have to trust yourself. You have to believe in your abilities and your strengths. If you don't believe in yourself, nobody will."

Hunter was right, and it was going to be hard to get used to that mindset. As much as it was nice to have Hunter helping me, I was an adult now and I needed to act that way.

Hunter continued to look through the box of work. For every piece of work he came across, he'd hold it up in the air to admire it and smile.

"The man I love is a genius," he said.

It made my body feel all fuzzy inside and blood rushed to my cheeks.

When he finally finished looking at everything that was inside, Hunter came up to kiss me. He lay back down on the bed next to me.

The sky had turned dark and there were no clouds that evening. Just an array of stars that twinkled over the skyline.

Hunter's hands moved over my body and I groaned at how great it felt to be touched by him.

We kissed under the stars and the city lights. I rolled on top of Hunter, straddling his thick legs.

I reached down to unbutton his shirt to expose his bare chest.

"Suck my nipples," he demanded.

I smiled and listened to him, putting his brown nipple in my mouth and sucking it gently. His groans filled the apartment and I was worried that my neighbors would hear. But Hunter didn't have a care in the world.

Hunter took my shirt off and I reached to unbutton his trousers.

"What underwear are you wearing today?" I asked, biting my lips.

"You'll see, baby."

It was like Christmas morning as I unzipped him, and I saw that he was wearing an old pair of green briefs. They were worn out and faded just like his other pairs. I put my face close to them to take in Hunter's intoxicating scent. I loved his underwear, it was always a pleasant surprise to see how confidently he wore them. It was also our little secret that beneath his expensive clothes, he always had on a bit of his past.

I pulled his grey trousers down and kept his briefs on. I could see the tip of his cock through one of the holes in his briefs and a bit of pre-come had leaked onto them.

Hunter kneeled on the bed and took off my athletic shorts. I pulled down my underwear along with it.

He pushed my body on the bed and started stroking me while looking into my eyes.

"I want to change things up tonight," he groaned.

Hunter lowered his head and put the tip of my cock in his mouth. It was the first time that he'd sucked my cock. His lips wrapped around my tip, and I felt his tongue swirl around it. He sucked me hard and deep, and I clawed onto his thick muscles.

He bobbed his head up and down while he squeezed my balls.

I never thought Hunter would ever be the one sucking me, but I knew he wanted to please me.

"You want to fuck me?" he asked, pausing for a moment with my cock still in his hands.

"Really? You want to bottom?" I asked.

"I want to try it with you, but more than anything, I want to see you take charge," he said.

My heart raced at the idea of being in the driver's seat when, for most of my life, I was happy just being the passenger. Hunter's seductive voice was convincing. The thought of being inside him made me that much harder.

"Okay," I said.

Hunter smirked and leaned forward to kiss me before lying down on the bed beside me.

26

HUNTER

I wasn't used to being in such a submissive position. I lay on Blue's bed with my legs pressed against my chest, exposing my most vulnerable part of my body to him. I had left my briefs on, and I'd worn this pair in particular that day for a reason.

"Are you going to take those off?" he asked.

I shook my head, and Blue looked down and knew why. There was a rip in my briefs right where my hole was.

"That's so fucking sexy," Blue said.

I smiled at him. "I knew it'd turn you on to fuck me with my briefs still on."

Blue's cock was big. Not as big as mine of course. I knew it would be difficult to take all of him, but I was determined to do it.

"Lube and condom?" Blue asked.

"Damn, I forgot we needed that," I said.

In my excitement, I'd forgotten that he couldn't just stick it in me.

"I didn't bring it," I said. "You don't have any?"

Blue shook his head, looking defeated.

"Well...I trust you," I said. "We don't need to use a condom if you're okay with it."

"I trust you too," Blue said. "But we still need lube."

I glanced over at the kitchen and saw a green bottle sitting on the counter.

"Can we use olive oil?" I asked.

"I've never done it before, but I'm sure it's possible," he said.

He got up from the bed and headed over to the kitchen and brought the bottle back to the bed. He took off the cap and rubbed some on his cock, then some on my ass.

"You're so hairy," he said.

I nodded. "It's a jungle down there, I know. I hope you don't mind."

"Not at all. I think it's sexy that your body is so different from mine."

I ran my hand on his smooth and toned torso, down to where his cock was, squeezing it in my hand.

"I'm ready for you, my love," I said. "I'm happy I get to share this experience with you."

"It's my first time topping too," Blue said.

I widened my eyes to get a better look at his face and saw that he was being serious.

"You've never fucked anyone before?" I asked to confirm.

"Nope, you're going to be the first. I've always been the bottom because of how I'm built, and because I enjoy taking a more submissive role."

Blue put some olive oil on his fingers that dripped onto his bed, and he rubbed my hole with it.

I closed my eyes, not used to being touched there for the first time. But Blue was gentle as he pushed his finger inside me.

"I think you're tighter than me," he said.

I grunted at the pressure of his finger.

"I don't know, you're pretty damn tight."

He pushed deeper inside of me, and I opened my eyes to see him smiling. That fucker was enjoying every moment of this.

He pulled out of me, and I grunted. I wanted more.

He stroked his cock several times before he aimed it on my hole.

"Ready?" he asked, leaning forward.

I put both my hands on his back and nodded, kissing his lips.

I felt the pressure of Blue's cock breaching my hole and I wanted to scream in pain.

I kissed his lips to distract me, as he wrapped his arms around my body, pushing deeper and deeper inside of me.

I took a deep breath when it felt like he'd slid his whole cock in and my body filled with warmth. It was a sensation that I'd never felt before.

I looked down to see how hard I was. My cock pulsed wildly against Blue's stomach.

I wrapped my thick legs around Blue's toned and narrow frame. The vibrations of his rhythmic thrusts felt incredible.

I moved my hands to cradle his face against my chest.

"That's it, baby, right there. I can't believe this is your first time topping," I groaned in his ear.

"And I can't believe this is your first time bottoming," he said. "You're taking me like a champ."

"I am a champion," I said. "And you're a trophy."

He lifted his face off my chest. There was a grin on his face when he grabbed my wrists to put them over my head, holding them there in place.

"You finally going to take charge?" I asked.

He nodded and I felt him thrust in me harder and quicker. It was so sexy to see how confident he was at that moment. I always knew he had it in him to take the lead. If getting fucked by Blue taught him to be more confident, I was willing to let him fuck my brains out.

Sweat covered our bodies as he quickened his pace.

"I'm going to come," he said.

I nodded and wrapped my legs tighter around him and he got the message of where I wanted him to shoot his load.

I felt his muscles tighten. I reached to stroke my cock as he pounded inside of me. In no time, I felt his warm come erupt inside my ass.

"God, baby," I groaned, stroking myself to my own climax. I came everywhere, covering our sweaty bodies and his sheets.

Blue collapsed onto me, his cock still pulsing inside my hole.

"You did it, handsome boy," I said, brushing back his wavy blond hair off his face.

I'd never seen Blue look as proud as he did at that moment.

Blue and I decided that he was going to start his new job as a design specialist in the creative department. I was excited to have him back in my firm, and I knew that we'd be able to accomplish great things together. I wanted Blue to continue to expand his creativity. I knew that he'd realize how satisfying it'd be to be doing what he loves. It was a lot better than doing something he wasn't passionate about.

Since Marie quit, I made more of an effort to get to know my employees. I was grateful to have them on my team. In the past, I'd only seen them as people who worked for me. But knowing that they supported me even after the scandal, I wanted to be more open and honest with them. I didn't want to hide out in my office all day and stay busy with work. I wanted to get to know everyone on a personal level.

I was sitting down with the creative department on my team

to go over some of the new work that they'd come up with. I took that chance to let them know that Blue was going to be starting later that week as a new member for the department.

At around seven in the evening, I walked over to Giorgio's restaurant. I had planned to meet Blue and his brothers there. Blue informed me that his oldest brother was also in town. I put on a big smile as I went into the restaurant. I noticed Blue's beautiful smile first and noticed Harry sitting next to him. A gentleman sat across from them, and I was surprised to see how much older he was than both of them.

I approached their table, and Blue stood up to greet me with a hug and a kiss.

In the past, I'd be uncomfortable with kissing him in public. But I no longer cared about what other people thought.

"I'm glad to see you," I whispered in Blue's ear. "It's been a long day."

I glanced over at Harry and shook his hand. "I'm surprised you decided to come back to this restaurant," I said, smiling at him. "I'm surprised they haven't banned you here after that fiasco."

"Definitely no drinks for you tonight," Blue added.

"I'll be fine," Harry said, slightly annoyed by my joke, but we both smiled at each other.

I knew that I'd have to get along with him for the sake of Blue.

I glanced over at the gentleman who was wearing a nice suit and sitting up straight.

"Hi, I'm Gray," he said.

He had a deep voice and, when he stood up, he was as tall as me.

"Nice to meet you, you must be Blue's oldest brother."

He nodded and smiled. There were a lot of similarities to Blue, he was handsome, and he had the same deep blue eyes. And his handshake was just as firm. I wondered if Blue was going to look like him when he was older.

I saw Giorgio in the kitchen.

"Giorgio," I called out. "Can we get some bottles of wine for these fine young gentlemen."

"Yes, sir, coming right up," Giorgio answered.

I sat down next to Blue and I squeezed his leg under the table to let him know how excited I was to get to meet his brothers.

The server came to bring over a bottle of white and red wine and filled our glasses. I needed that drink after a long day at work.

"What do you do?" Gray, who was sitting directly across from me, asked.

"I'm the CEO of a marketing company...and also Blue's boyfriend," I said, taking a sip of wine. "And you?"

"I'm a lawyer, working overseas currently in Hong Kong."

"That's great," I said. "I'd been looking to expand my business overseas."

Gray and I talked about what cases he'd been working on and the challenges of working in a foreign place. I was surprised at how much he reminded me of Blue. A more mature version, but equally talented in his own way.

"Why are you back in Toronto?" I asked Gray.

"To see this kid," he said, nodding in Blue's direction. "I came back when I found out he was in the hospital. I thought it was more serious, but I'm just glad he's okay."

"He's in good hands," I said. "I'll take good care of him."

Gray nodded, taking a sip of wine. "You seem like a pretty stand-up guy and it seems you'll help Blue be more disciplined."

I winked at Blue who was glaring at Gray like a younger brother would.

As always, we were served a delicious meal by Giorgio,

and I was glad to be surrounded by good company that evening. Talking to both Harry and Gray gave me a better sense of who Blue really was. He had a bit of both of his brothers in him, Gray's intelligence, and a bit of Harry's stubbornness.

At the end of dinner, Gray and I exchanged business cards.

We stood outside the restaurant as we waited for our rides.

Gray's Uber had arrived first. He turned to me to shake my hand.

"It was a pleasure to meet you tonight," Gray said. "I'm confident that you'll be good to my younger bro."

I nodded. "I will, don't worry. Have a safe flight back to Hong Kong."

"If you need anything, give me a call. You're family now," Gray said.

I smiled, knowing that Gray and I will cross paths soon despite how far he lived currently.

Harry hadn't been drinking that evening, so he was okay to drive home.

He reached out to shake my hand, but I opted to hug him instead.

"I know we have our differences," I said to him. "But I want you to know that I'm not like the guy who's hurt Blue in the past."

"I know," Harry said. "I know because I made it hard for you to see if you'd pass the test."

I had a newfound respect for Harry. The more time I spent to get to know him, the more I realized that he had many great qualities that even I could learn from.

Harry went over to Blue to ruffle up his hair, which made Blue pout in the most adorable way.

"Stay out of trouble, twerp," he said to Blue.

Harry went into his pickup and drove off. We stood outside the quiet streets of the restaurant. I was reminded of the night when I helped Blue and Harry get home. The summer nights were cooling down, but the heat between Blue and me had only just begun.

"Why don't we walk home tonight?" I suggested.

"Back to mine?" Blue asked.

"Yeah, I could use a bit of exercise after that meal."

I held my hand out to hold Blue's, and we locked our fingers with each other.

"I noticed that you were a bit tense earlier tonight when you arrived at the restaurant. Is everything okay?"

I glanced over at the concern in his eyes.

"Just a bit of stress meeting your family," I said. "There's nothing to worry about."

"Oh," Blue said. "Why were you nervous about that?"

We took a shortcut through a winding path that cut through a park.

"Because I love you," I said, pausing under a streetlamp. "And I wanted to make a good impression on Gray."

"I love you, too," Blue said. "You did great. I could see how you really clicked with Gray."

I leaned in to kiss his lips that tasted sweet from the red wine.

I smiled. Blue was the person I needed to tell me that there was still good in this world. He was there to give me the perspective I needed.

Holding his hand, and walking down the empty streets, I knew that I'd made the right decision. Despite challenges ahead, I was ready to face them with Blue by my side.

I took a deep breath as we made our way toward Blue's apartment. No matter what happened next, I was happy to have him in my life even if it meant having nothing else at all.

EPILOGUE

BLUE

Six Weeks Later

I stood outside the boardroom with the presentation boards in my hand. It was the first time I was presenting something in front of a potential client that Hunter had trusted me with. I wiped the sweat off my hands trying not to get the boards wet.

Hunter had said that he was going to be with me during this meeting. But he was running late from another meeting that was halfway across the city. Since I'd met Hunter, he'd been constantly pushing me outside my comfort zone. Though I hated presentations and meetings, he assured me that I was going to be okay.

The boardroom door opened, and a man with salt-and-pepper hair wearing a blue suit shook my hand.

"Hello, you must be Blue," he said. "Corey here."

I nodded and shook his hand.

"It's nice to meet you, Corey," I said, swallowing the lump in my throat and reminding myself to breathe.

Corey was the CEO of the company.

"You're a lot...younger than I expected," Corey said.

I smiled. "Young, but the best person for the job."

"I like your confidence," he said.

We stepped inside, and he introduced me to his three other colleagues. I shook their hands and I set up my presentation on the boardroom table in front of them.

I cleared my throat and went into my pitch. It was for a toy company who was trying to rebrand themselves to be more current with today's kids. I showed them the new logos that I designed.

I could tell that they were interested by how they were leaning forward in their chairs. The executives took a closer look at the designs that I'd been working on. This was my first project since Hunter had moved me into the creative department.

"Very interesting," Corey said, smiling. "I can see why you were put in charge of this. What you brought forward is exactly what we're looking for."

I smiled.

"We're looking forward to working with you. We want to create a larger online presence as well," Corey said.

They discussed amongst themselves on which concept they liked the most. We talked further about how I'd come up with these logos.

As the meeting went on, I got more comfortable and I understood why Hunter was so adamant about getting me to do this. By the time I left, I was beaming with excitement. I called Hunter as soon as I stepped outside of the meeting.

"Hey, how'd it go?" Hunter answered.

"Amazing, they really like it," I said. "I think they want to work with us!"

"That's great news! I'm on my way home from my meeting. I was wondering if you wanted to stop by for a little celebration."

I smirked. "What kind of celebration do you have in mind?"

"Well, a special one in bed, if you catch my drift."

"I'd love to, but I want to head back to the office to tell the team about how well it went. I'm sure they'd want to know," I said, waiting for the streetcar to head back to the office.

"Wow, since when did you start working harder than me?"

"Since you moved me to the creative side. I can't let my team down."

"You're right and I'm glad they liked it. I'm a bad influence."

"Why don't I see you at the office, we will have to hold off on the *celebration* until we get home tonight."

"Knowing how late we both work, it will probably have to wait until midnight," Hunter sighed.

"Well, I'm excited to see you anyway."

I went back to the office and members of my new team were hard at work on some new designs.

"Blue, you're back," Sophie, one of my fellow designers, greeted.

"I am! I Want to let you guys know that everything went well. We'll be hearing from them shortly about working with them."

I gave them all high fives and they beamed with excitement. I never thought I could be a part of something that was bigger than myself. This job was something I was passionate about every single day. Hunter had given me this opportunity to prove to myself that I was able to have a career that I loved.

I went back to my office, which was actually Marie's old office. The days of feeling like I had no control over my life were over, and it was just the beginning of my future with Hunter. We complemented each other's strengths and weaknesses.

As I was answering some emails, Hunter had snuck up on me. He was peering in through the doorframe watching me work.

"You're sneaky," I said.

"My bad, just love watching my boyfriend work," he said, walking in and closing the door behind him.

I opened my arms and Hunter leaned in for a hug and a kiss. I could never get over his rugged fresh scent.

"It's nice that you have an office now. So I can come in whenever I want to talk to you with some privacy," Hunter said, leaning against my desk.

His bulge was directly in my line of sight and I had a hard time paying attention to what I was typing. It was hard to stay professional around Hunter.

"You better behave yourself in here," I said. "Or we're going to get ourselves in another sticky situation again."

"Speaking of that, I just talked to Gray who had really great news for me."

For the past few weeks, my brother Gray has been helping Hunter to get connections overseas. Hunter was looking to expand his business in Asia.

"How's he doing? I haven't talked to him in a while," I said.

"First of all, I want to start off by saying, I love you and your family," Hunter said, smiling. "And second of all, he has very great news."

"What is it?" I asked.

"Well, it looks like we'll be landing our first project in Asia soon!"

"No way! Is that why you wanted to celebrate?"

"Yes! I want to give your brother a gift. Maybe we can fly out to see him on our honeymoon, I've always wanted to go to Hong Kong."

I leaned back in my chair, my eyes rounded. "Honeymoon? We never even talked about getting married."

"You're right." Hunter grinned, putting his finger to touch my chin. "We haven't talked about that yet, but I know I'm going to propose to you sooner or later. Just waiting on the right moment, that's all."

My heart raced at the idea of taking Hunter's last name and being with him forever.

"I love you," I said.

"I love you, too," Hunter said. "I'll let you get back to work, I don't want to distract you any further. But let's go out to dinner tonight to celebrate. We have a lot to be grateful about."

"Let's make a reservation at Giorgio's restaurant tonight," I said.

"That way, we can promise each other to get off at a reasonable hour tonight. How's six thirty sound?"

"Let's make it six," Hunter said, leaning forward to brush his nose against mine. "We need to save some time for the real celebration at home tonight."

I winked at him and pushed him away playfully. "Alright, well you better get back to work then or else neither of us is getting to the restaurant on time."

We shared one quick kiss before he left my office. The past few months hadn't been easy. Marie leaving his company after ten years had really messed up the structure. I was glad things were falling into place and that we could finally leave it behind us. There was a lot to be thankful for. I reminded myself every day how fortunate I was to be in this position, doing what I loved with the man I loved. I also had two brothers who supported me along the way even though one was overseas.

The thought of marriage had crossed my mind many times. Since dating Hunter, I started to believe in love again. The past tribulations I had with my ex felt like a very distant memory. I trusted Hunter and I believed that I could face any problems in the future with him. I felt safe with Hunter, and most importantly, I felt confident.

I finished the rest of my work. At the end of the day, I went upstairs to Hunter's office to get him for dinner.

He was busy on the phone, but he smiled as soon as I walked in.

"Listen, I have to go," he said with one hand on his phone. "I have a very important person to attend to."

He hung up and came up to me to kiss me.

"Ready to go?" I asked.

"I'm always ready when it's with you."

We headed down to the elevator. Hunter couldn't keep his hands off me. He touched me all over my body, kneading my ass with his big and strong hands.

"Control yourself," I whispered.

"I'm trying, I spend most of my day thinking about you and when I finally get to see you, it's impossible not to touch you."

I put my hands on his rugged jaw and pulled him in for a kiss before the elevator doors opened.

It didn't feel like summer anymore. The sticky humid days were behind us. Fall was approaching. We were bracing for the long Canadian winter. That meant hibernating in bed on evenings and weekend, which neither Hunter nor I were going to mind.

We walked across the street to the restaurant, and though it was a bit chilly out, the tables on the patio were full.

We stepped inside, feeling the heat from the kitchen. Giorgio caught a glimpse of us as he was preparing a drink behind the bar for a patron.

"Look who it is. My two favorite customers," Giorgio said.

We smiled and waved at him, then one of his servers sat us by the window.

I looked out at the darkening sky. Days were getting shorter which had always depressed me before. But it didn't seem to matter now, because I never had to worry about being alone at night with Hunter around.

The server brought us our favorite bottle of red wine and poured us two glasses.

Hunter and I clinked our glasses together and the wine warmed my body.

"I never thought someone could make me this happy," Hunter said, looking right into my eyes.

Blood rushed to my cheeks. I still had a hard time getting compliments from Hunter because I knew how deeply he meant it.

"I never thought someone would make me smile so much that my cheeks hurt," I said.

"Well, it's a good look on you when you're smiling, so I hope I will always make you feel this way."

"As long as I'm with you, I'll always feel special."

"Well, you are special. You make me into a better man."

He reached forward to hold onto my hands. Though the restaurant was full, Hunter didn't mind kissing them. He'd gotten over his fear of other people seeing who he truly was. That was one thing that made me so proud of him. From the way he was holding my hand, I knew that Hunter was going to be holding on to me forever.

EXCLUSIVE LOOK

HARRY'S BABY (EVERETT BROS BOOK 2)

HARRY'S BABY

THE EVERETT BROS BOOK 2

Harry: We were friends, then roommates, now…a baby?

Carter and I started off as *just friends* who were heading up north to work at a lucrative mining job. But after a few beers one night, a fire ignited between us that neither of us knew how to put out.

Yes, I'm straight.

But Carter somehow manages to make me question it. I guess being gay—or bi…whatever you wanna call it—might run in the Everett family.

Carter: I always pictured myself being a dad. But not like this…

On my 40th birthday, I realized something—all my friends were married with kids. Me? I still lived the life of a bachelor and it was getting old quick. I guess you can call it a mid-life crisis.

Harry came into my life as nothing more than just a friend. Let me say one thing, though. Redheads are definitely my type. But even though I've experimented with guys before, I wasn't expecting to be falling *this hard* for a man.

An accident at work leaves me and Harry with an orphaned baby. Can two men who know nothing about fatherhood figure this thing out… *together?*

Warning: Harry's Baby contains explicit sexual content not suitable for anyone under the age of 18.

The Everett Bros focuses on three brothers who go on their own journeys to find love. Each novel in The Everette Bros series can be read on its own or as part of the series.

1

HARRY

My life has been kind of shitty since the beginning. Now that my brother Blue had moved out of my one-bedroom apartment, I felt even lonelier than before. I was twenty-seven, and life seemed to be only getting worse.

I lay on the couch flipping through the channels trying to find something to watch. I was debating between baseball highlights of the game that I just watched or the tennis match. The television was a way to distract me from the fact that it was already very late and I had to go to work the next day. My only day off that week was yet again spent lying on my couch and without anything meaningful to do.

In the kitchen, pizza boxes that I hadn't thrown out yet were stacked on top of each other. Next to it was a pile of bills that

I hadn't paid. At twenty-seven, I knew I had to get my shit together. But it was difficult to get motivated and do something about my life when there was so little to look forward to. Maybe two days off in a row if I was lucky? Or maybe I'd catch a break and finally win that lottery jackpot that I'd been playing into for the last few years. I had come close one time, missing the jackpot by only one number. Somehow, it only netted me a free ticket and a hundred bucks.

I looked at the clock above the television, and I saw that it was already nine, and I hadn't left the house that day. So I sluggishly got up and decided to take the pizza boxes out to the trash, ignoring the bills next to it. The hallways smelled of marijuana as I stepped outside. One of my neighbors was just coming up the stairs holding bags of groceries in each hand.

"Mr. Walker," I said, putting the pizza boxes on the floor. "Let me help you with that."

I walked briskly towards him and took the groceries from his frail hands. I wondered how old he was. Mr. Walker was always hunched forward. Seeing him like that always made me stand up a bit taller in fear that I'd become hunched like him one day.

"Thank you, Harry. You're a kind soul." He smiled while fumbling for his keys.

"What in the world did you buy at the grocery store? This is enough food to last you weeks!" I said as we walked down the hallway.

"Well, the deals were just too good today," he said. "And you know I can't turn down a good deal."

I smiled as I watched him fish his keys out of his pocket and tried to find the one to his door.

I was curious to ask why he had so many keys. But I figured that asking him that would be unwise. There was a possibility of him going on a long tangent about which each key led to. He made at least four attempts before finding the right one. My arms were starting to ache from the weight of the groceries.

Finally, he opened the door to his dark apartment. Our units were next to each other. They were the same size, except his was so cluttered that I could barely see any of the walls at all.

"It's a bit messy here," he said.

A bit?

He said that every time I had to help him with something, and the piles and piles of things were only getting higher. It would take a team of people to clean this place up. I worried about what would be under all those things.

"Where do you want your groceries?" I asked.

"Just by the fridge is fine," Mr. Walker said.

I looked around, trying to spot where exactly that was, and traced the path for me to get there. Navigating through the mess was like walking through a maze. I tried my best to make sure I didn't fall and cause an earthquake from everything toppling over.

"Careful about not stepping on Sneezy," he said.

"Oh right, the cat," I said, scanning the ground for moving objects. It was like a minefield in here. By the time I made it to the kitchen, I was sweating.

I set the groceries next to the fridge.

"Here is fine?" I asked.

Mr. Walker nodded, hanging his hat on the wall.

"Why do you keep so many things in here, Mr. Walker?" I asked.

"Well, a lot of people throw away things that are in perfect condition. It's a shame because if I had more space, I could salvage more of it."

I glanced around the room, seeing stacks of dated magazines. The covers were faded and worn out. Monitors that looked like they were from the nineties. Cans of tomato soup that stacked high on top of each other like a Warhol painting.

"Well, when there's too much of anything, it starts becoming...a bit less valuable," I said.

I fumbled over my worlds because I didn't want to hurt his feelings. The last thing I wanted to do was give him more weight on his back making him hunch even more if that was even possible.

"You're right, Harry," he said. "I'll clean this up first thing tomorrow!"

He'd said that many times before, but it only got worse. I figured it was no use, and I had done my job to carry his groceries inside.

"Do you want to stay for some tea?" Mr. Walker asked. "I have this new lemon green tea that's magnificent. If only I could remember where I put it..."

"Not tonight, Mr. Walker. I shouldn't have any caffeine before bed, or I'll stay up all night. I have work tomorrow."

"Ahh, work! Well, I shouldn't keep you any longer, then."

I smiled and walked towards the door.

"Don't work too hard," Mr. Walker said.

I paused at the door and turned to him.

"What do you mean by that?" I asked.

"When you're my age, you'll know what I mean. But in the meantime, just take my word for it. Don't you have a girl-friend? I never see you bring any ladies home."

I felt blood rush to my cheeks, and I wondered if it looked as red as my hair.

"No girlfriend," I said. "Haven't had one in years."

"Oh, are you one of those homosexuals?"

I smiled. "Nope, not gay either. But my brother Blue is. You've met him before."

"Ahh yes, he lived with you briefly. He was a fine young gentleman."

Mr. Walker's cat, Sneezy, appeared from the shadows, and it scared the shit out of me. I jumped back, knocking against a stack of milk crates filled with mason jars. I had to turn to steady them quickly before they toppled over.

"Jesus, Sneezy, give a warning next time before you just appear out of nowhere," I said.

Mr. Walker reached down to pick her up, and the cat yawned and nudged her head against Mr. Walker's pale neck.

"I'm going to head out now," I said. "Better get to bed, or I'll be tired at work."

"All right, Harry. Take care," Mr. Walker said, smiling.

I stepped back out to the hallway and closed the door. I rubbed my eyes to adjust to the brightness of the fluorescent lights.

I was reminded of the pizza boxes that I still had to take out. I picked them up off the ground and brought them downstairs to the garbage bins. I lived on the second floor, so it was only one flight of stairs down. I was wearing a white tank top and a pair of athletic shorts. The summer evening breeze brushed against my cock. I hadn't had sex in so long that even a bit of wind was capable of giving me a semi-hard-on. I hoped that I wasn't going to run into any more neighbors who could see me sporting a boner.

When Mr. Walker asked me if I had a girlfriend, I was reminded of how single I was. Single, not in a good way. *A good kind of single* was being out and having a good time, meeting and fucking new girls every night. But that wasn't the case for me. I'd never had that *good kind of single* type of life. People told me that I was handsome and tall, and they were right about one thing. At six foot one, I was very tall. But being tall didn't equate to having good game with the ladies, and when it came to that, I was awkward as fuck. I guess it stemmed from being teased for my red hair my whole life. I'd even buzzed it once, but it'd only made it appear even redder when it was that short. I spent most of my teenage years and early twenties playing baseball and watching sports. People rarely saw me without a baseball cap. I made sure of hiding my hair so that people couldn't call me names like daywalker. It had once angered me so much in high school that I'd gotten into a fistfight.

I worked in construction, mostly because I was strong, and a helmet allowed me to cover up my hair. I knew that it was irrational to have that insecurity, but I'd never grown out of it. I was twenty-seven, and I was strong enough to beat anyone up that bothered me. No one had called me a daywalker in years, but that still didn't make me hate my red hair any less. Both of my brothers were blond. Why couldn't I have just been like them?

Throwing out the pizza boxes was enough productivity for a day off. I sat on the ledge outside of my apartment to take in the fresh air and the quietness that I'd always loved at night.

When I headed back upstairs to my unit, I heard Mr. Walker talking to his cat in his apartment. The walls were thin in this apartment. I was glad that I wasn't having any wild sex—*or any sex at all for that matter.* Because my neighbors, and especially Mr. Walker, would be able to hear everything. It was a bit sad to see how lonely Mr. Walker seemed, and I wondered if anyone thought that way about me. But did anyone care anyway? It wasn't like I had many friends who thought about me or anything.

I went back into my apartment and straight to my bedroom, turning on the air conditioner that sat in my window. I stripped out of my clothes and set my alarm on my phone. It was going to be another long day on the jobsite, and the summer heat wasn't going away anytime soon. I only wished that I worked nights instead. Working nights would let me sleep all day. Since I only ever left my apartment at night anyway, it would fit perfectly with my schedule.

I lay naked on my sheets as the air conditioning cooled my room.

I went into one of the trailers on-site and put my lunch in the fridge. I'd showed up a bit later than I should. It was after my day off, so I was feeling particularly sluggish. It didn't help that it was one of the hottest days of the year. Even stepping outside for one second made me sweat. It was going to be a long one, a twelve-hour shift, with a possibility of overtime. I wouldn't know until the end of the day if I had to work more hours. It was just the way that things worked around here.

"Harry!" someone called out.

I turned to see who had said my name, and sure enough, it was one of the guys on my team.

"Carter, you're in a good mood today, for a Monday," I said, stretching my arms out to let out a big yawn.

"Well, every day's a great day on the jobsite," he said with a sarcastic smirk.

"You're shitting me," I said. "I've never seen you look so excited unless it's before a long weekend."

Carter had dark hair that I envied and tan skin from working outside in construction. I'd only managed to get more freckles. He was one of the taller guys, six foot five, and I figured he was almost ten years older than me as well. If I remembered correctly, he turned forty last month.

"I am shitting you. But I am happy for a reason," Carter said.

He came up to me and squeezed me on the shoulder so hard that it felt numb afterwards.

"And what's that reason?" I asked.

"I'm not sure if I can tell you right now. But I can after work. We can meet at the Tim Horton's down the street or something," he said, pushing me aside to open the door to the fridge. He put his lunch bag in the vegetable crisper drawer, which I thought was weird.

"Fine," I said.

"We better get going," Carter said. "We'll get yelled at again for being late."

I looked at the time and nodded. We walked quickly to where

the rest of the guys were. They were standing under a large concrete slab that we had just put up. The team leader, Brad, was holding construction plans in one of his hands. He faced a group of ten guys. Cigarette smoke filled the air. I thought it was a gross habit. Though I picked it up when I first started working here because I was surrounded by it all the time. I'd quit for over five years now, and I was feeling much healthier.

"What's the holdup? You boys jerking off in the break room?" Brad shouted.

Everyone on the crew burst out in laughter, staring at Carter and me. I pulled my helmet over my eyes.

"Yes, sir, but we couldn't find a photo of your wife to finish," Carter shouted back.

The crew laughed even harder, including me, and Brad was the one who looked uncomfortable now.

"Good one," I whispered as I nudged Carter's arm.

"Settle down, everyone," Brad said. "We are getting down to crunch time. If we aren't going to finish on time, know that none of your contracts are getting renewed."

I hated how he always used threats as a way to scare us. Most days, Brad was hanging out with his other team leader buddies while we were doing all the work. It pissed me off that there was nothing I could do about it. We were unionized, and I knew that getting laid off wasn't as cut and dry as Brad made it out to be. But other guys on the team, some with families and children, took him more seriously.

Brad went through the goals for the day, and he delegated responsibilities to us.

"Carter and Harry, since you joined us late today, I am putting you two on the loading dock."

Both Carter and I grunted at the thought of doing the hardest part on this site.

"You got to be kidding me," I whispered to Carter.

"You have something to say about it?" Brad asked.

Brad had a handlebar mustache that screamed *douchebag*. He puffed out his chest when he spoke like he was a tough guy when, really, he was the shortest person on the team.

"No," I said, lowering my head.

I didn't want any more confrontation, and I guess the silver lining was getting to work with Carter, who I didn't mind.

"Good. Now get to it," Brad said.

We dispersed, and Carter and I made it over to the shipping container that we had to unload. There was an insane amount of dust when I opened the doors. The shipping container was filled with concrete blocks, and each one had to be moved manually.

"Another day, another paycheck," Carter said.

"I guess so," I said.

It was depressing to have to do this mundane and repetitive task, but I guess it could have been a lot worse.

"Hold your head up, Harry," Carter said, smiling. "The day isn't going to be any easier if you're upset about it."

"You have a point," I said. "But I still don't know what you have to tell me that's putting you in such a good mood."

"You'll see," he said. "Just know that I got you."

It was reassuring to know that I had one person who at least appeared to be my friend on the jobsite. Carter stood on the bed of the shipping container while I remained on the ground. One by one, he passed the concrete blocks down to me, and I stacked them on a wooden skid. The sun was beating down hard. It wasn't even noon yet when it would be the hottest time of the day during the hottest day of the year. Sweat glistened on my freckled skin. I tried to distract myself from my aching arms by thinking about what Carter had to tell me. I imagined different scenarios. Maybe he was getting married. Maybe he'd won the lottery, and he was going to retire. Either way, I tried whatever I could to escape the moment.

I glanced over at Brad, who was standing under the shade of one of the trailers. His irritating laugh could be heard from a mile away. He was looking over at Carter and me, and I could only assume that he was making a stupid daywalker joke to his buddies.

2

CARTER

There were two things getting me through the day, and one of those things was getting to work with Harry. Out of all the guys on-site, I seemed to click with him the most, and maybe it was because I sensed that he was an outcast like me. He was a good guy, and he worked hard, but he was awful with people.

We were assigned the hardest task on-site, and the task was only made harder by the harsh sun. The concrete dust that was covering my body shielded against the rays. Sweat trickled down my forehead onto my back.

"What's the time?" I asked.

Harry grunted as he fished into his pocket to pull out his phone.

"Twenty minutes until lunch," he said.

I smiled, already feeling the rumble in my stomach. Time on-site was only relative to lunchtime or until the end of the day. So naturally, people told the time based on when those things were approaching. Brad never seemed to like me, and I had no idea why. I stood one foot taller than him, so I figured maybe it had to do with his Napoleon complex. Since getting assigned to his team, work hadn't been enjoyable.

I watched as he approached us. His beer gut jutted out, and even the way he walked annoyed me.

"How many skids to go?" Brad asked.

I looked into the nearly empty shipping container to try and estimate.

"Looks like we have just a few more," I said.

"A few more?" Brad repeated. "Well, better get them finished before you leave for lunch."

"What? Can't we do them after?" Harry asked, wiping the sweat and dust off his forehead.

"Nope, gotta finish first. We have to clear this empty container out as soon as possible."

Harry and I glanced at each other. We were aware of Brad's bullshit, but we were powerless over his decision. His mind was most likely already made up when I gave him lip that morning. I should've known better than to be a smartass about it, but sometimes I found it hard to keep my mouth shut. Especially if things seemed unfair.

We watched as our entire crew went into the trailers for lunch. Every one of them taking off their helmets to go into the air-conditioned space.

"Goddammit, Carter. If this isn't hell on earth, I certainly have no interest in finding out what hell is like."

I smiled, opening my bottle of water, which I kept next to a rock to keep it shaded and cooled.

"Relax, Harry. Just look at it as a challenge. You'll only grow stronger from it," I said.

"I wish I could see things with your rose-colored glasses. I don't know what you're going on about, but I certainly am ready to eat my slice of pizza, which I put in the fridge."

The thought of pizza made me hungrier. I flicked the bottle of water gently towards Harry, and it soaked the front of his white T-shirt and a bit on his face.

"Cut it out," he said.

But I did it again. This time it splashed against his neck.

"I mean it, Carter. I'm already soaked from sweat," he said with his red brows furrowed.

"Okay, okay, chill out, man. I'm just trying to lighten things up. Besides, Brad isn't out here hovering over our shoulders," I said.

"He'd have to be on stilts for him to be tall enough to do that," he said.

I laughed so hard that I snorted some of the water.

"There we go," I said, smiling at Harry's joke. "I didn't think you were such a funny guy."

I climbed back onto the bed of the truck to grab another tray of bricks.

"I'm not even that funny, but how can you not crack jokes at our shitty supervisor."

"You're right," I said. "And I hope something changes soon."

When we finally finished, people were already returning from lunch.

We went towards the trailer, and Brad was holding the door open to let people out.

"You boys have fifteen minutes," Brad said. "We'll need you out here as soon as you're done eating."

Harry looked at Brad with his bright green eyes, and I swear he looked so angry that he was going to punch Brad out. I saw his fists clench, and I put a hand on Harry's shoulder to try and snap him out of it.

We headed into the cooled break room.

"It's not too bad that we had to wait," I said. "Now we don't have to listen to the other guys' pervy jokes."

"I guess you're right," Harry said, heading right for the fridge.

I watched him stick his head in the fridge to cool down, but when he started swearing, I knew something was wrong.

"Some fucker took my lunch," he said.

"Goddammit, are you serious?" I looked inside to see if mine was still there. I'd known to put it in the vegetable crisper drawer where I knew people wouldn't find it easily.

"Rookie mistake, Harry," I said. "Everyone knows that pizza always gets stolen."

As if he wasn't already pissed, he was looking even angrier now.

"I bet Brad ate it," he said.

"You're probably right," I said.

I opened up my lunch bag and took out one of my two sandwiches and tossed one over to Harry.

"Consider yourself lucky today," I said.

Harry grabbed the sandwich that was in a Ziploc bag. "You sure?"

"I'm sure," I said. "The last thing I want to do is work the rest of the shift with you if you're hungry. We both know that neither of us will get much done."

I was a big guy, and I knew that I needed both sandwiches to get me through that shift. But we were a team, and Harry needed it more than me.

We took a seat at the table where the supervisors and team leads usually sat. It was under the air-conditioning vent, which was why it was the best table.

I watched as Harry took a bite of the sandwich and closed his eyes to savor the bite.

"Good?" I asked, opening my sandwich up as well.

"Amazing. What's in it?" he asked.

"Cucumber and cream cheese, my all-time favorite combo," I said.

"Did your wife make it?" he asked.

"Wife?" I repeated. "What makes you think I'm married."

"I don't know. Guys here usually are, so I just kind of assumed," Harry said.

"I'm happily single," I said, kicking my boots off under the table to really sink back in the plastic chair. "What about you?"

I was bi, and I hated sharing my sexuality at work.

"I'm single. Don't know if I'm that happy about it though," Harry said.

"You're a good-looking guy. Don't you have luck with the ladies?" I asked.

"Not at all. I'm more like a chick repellant," Harry said.

I chuckled, taking another huge bite of my sandwich. I was already halfway finished.

"That's surprising to me. Maybe I can teach you some lessons on how to up your game," I said.

Harry laughed. "And what makes you the expert?"

"Good point. It's been a while since I've had the energy to go out and chase someone like I used to back in my college days."

I didn't mention that they were usually guys that I was chasing.

"College?" he asked.

"Yeah, I was an honor-roll student."

"Damn, why the hell are you in a dead-end construction job?" he asked.

"Well, I graduated from architecture, and it was during a recession. I looked everywhere for some work related to my field, but I had no luck. Construction happened to be the first job that I found."

"Why'd you stop looking?" he asked.

Harry had finished the sandwich, and he walked over to the coffee machine that was on the counter next to the sink.

"I just got too comfortable, I guess. Construction, though it sucks sometimes, paid the bills. I was a bit worried that if I ever left it, I'd end up screwing myself over."

Harry brought over two cups of coffee and gave one to me.

"You're smarter than all the guys here. I bet that if you really wanted to, you could find something that wasn't so shitty."

"You have a point, Harry," I said, taking a sip of coffee. "It might be too late now, though. It's been years since I've done any architectural work. Nowadays, firms are probably using computer programs that I'd never even heard of."

I looked over at Harry, who was pushing his Styrofoam cup on the table from one hand to the other.

"What's on your mind?" I asked.

"Nothing," he said, but I remained silent for him to continue. "It's just that I wished I went to college like my brothers. Then maybe I'd be able to...*be someone.*"

"What did you do after high school?" I asked.

"I did a victory lap to continue to play baseball, hoping I'd get scouted to join a college team."

"And what happened?" I asked.

"I tore my hamstring early in the season, and everything was ruined after that. I was banking on that plan. Now here I am. I wish that my younger self would've thought long and hard about trying to be a pro baseball player." Harry sighed. "Like I even had a chance to begin with."

I felt sorry for the guy. Seeing his shoulders rounded forward and the pain in his voice made me want to get up and give him a hug. But there was no man-to-man contact on the jobsite, or else we'd never hear the end of it.

"Look, I wanted to wait until the end of the day to tell you, but I guess I can let you know now," I said.

"What is it?" Harry asked, looking up at me.

"I know a friend who told me about this opportunity if you're up for it."

"Go on," Harry said leaning forward.

"You can't tell anyone though, because it's not for certain yet. But if I get it, I'm pretty certain that I'm leaving this shithole."

Harry's eyes widened, looking as if he was dying to know what I was about to tell him.

"My friend told me about an opportunity up north. They're hiring nickel miners. It's a four-month task, but in those four months, we'll be making double of what we would make in a year here," I said.

"Nickel mining, isn't that dangerous?" he asked.

"It is, but my friend said it's worth it. It's not like this job is all that safe anyway."

"Where is the job?" Harry asked, his green eyes glowing in the midafternoon sun.

"Thunder Bay," I said.

"Thunder Bay...that's far from here," Harry said, putting his hand on his chin and stroking it.

"If you're interested, I can tell my friend, and we can head up together. That way it will be easier than going alone. I think it's a really great opportunity. If you ever want to get back into construction, you can get a similar job when you get back."

"So, it's four months, and that's it?" he asked.

I nodded. "What do you say, Harry? Want to take the risk with me? I think it will be fun. We know that we both hate it here, so we really have nothing to lose."

Just as I said that, the front door of the trailer swung open.

"I hate to interrupt the little date that you have going on here," Brad said. "But I said fifteen minutes!"

"Okay," I said. "We'll be out in a second."

I glanced back over at Harry, who looked like he was seriously considering my offer.

"Let me think about it," Harry said.

HARRY'S BABY

(THE EVERETT BROS BOOK 2)

Amazon Link:

Harry's Baby (The Everett Bros Book 2)

ALSO BY CANDICE BLAKE

Single Dads Club

DAMON (Book 1)

Beckford Brothers

LEO (Book 1)

KINGSTON (Book 2)

CHRISTIAN (Book 3)

SAINT (Book 4)

The Everett Bros

Blue's Boss (Book 1)

Harry's Baby (Book 2)

Gray's Playroom (Book 3)

Billionaires of Forest Hill (Mpreg)

The Omega's Bodyguard (Book 1)

The Omega's Protector (Book 2)

The Omega's Savior (Book 3)

The Omega's Doctor (Book 4)

Standalones

A Road Trip with Conrad

Kings of Hearts

Encore

Chase

Lost in Nomad's Land

Men of the Atlantic

Jay to December (Book 1)

Remy by the Sea (Book 2)

ABOUT THE AUTHOR

Candice Blake is an author of gay romance.

For more information, visit
candiceblake.com

NEWSLETTER

Sign up for Candice's Newsletter to get the latest updates!

Thanks for reading <3

Printed in Great Britain
by Amazon

27337812R00189